The two cars in front of Kris took the third turn and headed into the straightaway, arrows aimed at Randall and Boyd, who were squatting like roadkill in the middle of the track. They had plenty of time to drive around them. Kris's view would be blocked until it was too late.

Kyle said, "Drop back, Kris, you're clear high."

In Kyle's mind the toy cars slowed so he could reach down and rearrange them. His mind touched the Blue Shadow.

He could almost feel Kris twist the wheel right and point the car toward the wall, the high side, spinning and slowing once there was no one ahead or behind. Sparks flew as he rubbed the wall, but he kept control and steered around Randall and Boyd.

"Thanks, little bro." He sounded like he meant it.

Kyle was jacked. For a moment there, he had felt inside the car, and that felt good.

YELLOW FLAG

ROBERT LIPSYTE

HARPER TEEN
An Imprint of HarperCollinsPublishers

HarperTeen is an imprint of HarperCollins Publishers.

Yellow Flag
Copyright © 2007 by Robert Lipsyte
For information address HarperCollins Children's Books, a division of HarperCollins
Publishers, 10 East 53rd Street, New York, NY 10022.
www.harperteen.com

Library of Congress Cataloging-in-Publication Data
Lipsyte, Robert.
    Yellow flag / Robert Lipsyte. — 1st ed.
        p.   cm.
    Summary: When seventeen-year-old Kyle reluctantly succumbs to family pressure and
replaces his injured brother in the family race car, he struggles to keep up with his trumpet
playing while deciding how—or if—he can continue making music with a brass quintet and
headline as a NASCAR racer.
    ISBN 978-0-06-055709-6 (pbk.)
    [1. Automobile racing—Fiction. 2. Trumpet—Fiction. 3. Family life—North Carolina—
Fiction. 4. Music—Fiction. 5. Self-actualization (Psychology)—Fiction. 6. North Carolina—
Fiction.] I. Title.
PZ7.L67Yel 2007   2006100438
[Fic]—dc22   CIP
                                                                                                AC

Typography by Larissa Lawrynenko
09 10 11 12 13   10 9 8 7 6 5 4 3 2 1
❖
First paperback edition, 2009

For my crew chief,
Ruth Katcher

YELLOW FLAG

ONE

He was coming off the last turn, racing three wide for the finish, Dad on his left, Kris on his right, trapped between them. Through the roar of the engines he heard the metallic shriek of their doors scraping. Uncle Kale's voice came through the headphones: "Gas it, Kylie, get out of there."

Kyle thought, If we cross the finish line together, I will never get out of this car. I will be stuck in here forever.

Even as he dreamed, he knew it was a dream, the old one, the yellow caution flag dream, the early warning dream. Something's going to happen today.

He forced himself awake the way he always did, braking hard, letting Dad and Kris pass him to the checkered flag. He was unstuck, free.

But he was nowhere.

He woke up sweating.

Be careful today.

Kyle wasn't surprised at breakfast when Dad said, "We could use you tomorrow."

He felt the orange juice come back up faster than it went down, pure acid. "Got a trumpet lesson. Then the quintet's going to Charlotte for a master class."

Dad's long face looked tired. He sounded apologetic. "I need you. Billy went to Atlanta for some heart tests."

Mom said, "You can reschedule your lesson." Kyle thought that was her way of saying, I'm not on your side this time.

"I wouldn't ask if it wasn't important," said Dad. "The new sponsors'll be there. Kris comes in top ten, we can make this deal."

The orange acid went back down and pooled in Kyle's stomach. Dad didn't have to say how bad Hildebrand Racing needed to make this deal.

Mom said, "I think you should do it." As if she were pleading with him to make the right choice.

That made it worse, Kyle thought, putting it all on me, as if I really had a choice. It was a con job. Pleading had never been the Hildebrand way. Great-grandpa

Fred ordered Grandpa Walter into the car, and then Walter ordered Dad into the car. Dad had never had to order Kris, who had jumped in when he was four years old. Never could get him out. Only reason I escaped.

"Need you up on the spotters' stand," said Dad. "Kris'll listen to you."

Yeah, right. Kris'll listen to me. And still push the pedal through the floor.

What could he say? "What time?"

"Knew I could count on you." Dad smiled. "We can drive out together after school."

No way. Miss rehearsal tonight and get stuck tomorrow three hours from home without my own car. "I'll go in the morning. Be there by nine."

Dad hesitated, but Mom said, "I'll make sure you're up." So she was half on his side.

Fridays in spring crept on forever at Goshen High. All day Kyle felt like he had one foot mashing the gas, the other standing on the brake. His motor was running hot while his wheels spun in the groove. Sweat ran down his back. He felt numb and horny and sleepy and jittery. He sleepwalked from English to history to geometry. He heard himself answer a question in environmental science, but it might as well have been someone else. Teachers droned on, trying not to let their eyes flick toward the windows, where the thickening yellow light banged against the glass, calling them outside. Kyle's eyes were stuck on the glass.

He didn't remember what he ate for lunch or who sat with him at the band table.

He didn't wake up until he tightened the thumbscrew on his music stand in the band practice room. He always woke up for practice. But he also started thinking about tomorrow. It wasn't fair. *Racing is Kris's life, not mine. I've got other things to do.*

"So why don't gorillas play trumpet?" He hadn't noticed Nicole sit down next to him. As usual, she was all in black. The little round face with big dark eyes peeked out of a cloud of curly black hair. She answered her own question. "Gorillas don't play trumpet because they're too sensitive."

"You know how French horn players say hello?" said Kyle. "They say, 'Hi, I played that piece in kindergarten.'" He liked trash talking with her, even the dumb old jokes.

She laughed. A big, unself-conscious sound. Behind her back some kids called it her New York honk, but he liked it better than the constipated simper that usually passed for laughs in Goshen.

"What's the difference between a trumpet player and a terrorist?" asked Jesse, lowering the twin pillows of his gargantuan butt onto his chair with a fat plop. "Terrorists have sympathizers."

Nicole laughed louder and Kyle felt a twinge of jealousy.

Mr. G bounced into the room in his plaid pajama pants and throwback Skechers, wearing yet another T-shirt from an obscure band. Molly's Brain Fart. Jesse and Nicole had made up a band name for him—Terminal Hip. He loved it, said he was going to have T-shirts made.

"Let's perpetrate some sound," he shouted.

They warmed up with Ravel's "Pavane for a Dead Princess," a beautiful piece they had played at the Charlotte Classical Festival last month. Kyle and the other trumpet, Todd, led them into the melody with quick bright sounds that opened doors for Del's tenor trombone. Mr. G nodded and pointed his baton, and they were surrounded by the warm, rich tones of Nicole's French horn and Jesse's tuba.

Kyle felt good for the first time all day. He felt safe and sure inside the music, working together with friends. He felt . . . complete.

As usual, it was over too quickly. Mr. G rapped his baton on a metal stand. "Okay, before we get serious, some business. One, who's driving tomorrow besides me?"

For a moment, Kyle was confused. Kris is driving tomorrow, in the Relco 250 at Monroe Speedway, and I'm going to be spotting for him on the roof.

"I can't make it," said Kyle.

"You are joking," said Mr. G. "You know how hard it was to get a high school quintet into a Brooklyn Brass master class?"

"I'm really sorry, but . . ."

"This better be good," said Mr. G. "You're having brain surgery."

It's a long story you wouldn't understand, smart-ass. My family needs me to help close a deal that will keep Hildebrand Racing alive. Pay my way to college. Pay for music lessons. Maybe you understand that. "I have to be at the track."

Mr. G's face got hard. "We've talked about this before, Kyle. The quintet's a commitment. You're on this team or you're not."

Del said, "It's not like we're going to play tomorrow." His family had raced; he understood.

Mr. G rolled his eyes. "Sooner or later you're going to have to make a decision, Kyle."

He let it hang in the air like a sour note. Kyle imagined telling Dad that he couldn't make the race.

No way.

Or telling Mr. G to go stick the baton.

Maybe later.

Kyle looked down and fussed with his spit valve. He felt a light punch on his arm. When he turned, Nicole was nodding at him. He wasn't totally sure what it meant, but he decided she was on his side.

TWO

"Imagine Mr. G naked and then try to eat your pizza," said Jesse, dramatically waving the hand that wasn't clutching pizza.

Nicole honked, and Jesse tapped his finger and thumb together in mocking applause for himself before returning to nibble delicately at his slice.

Kyle tore off a piece of his slice with his front teeth. It was past eleven P.M. They'd been jamming for more than three hours in Del's rec room. Have to go home soon and get some sleep, but he hadn't wanted to break up the session. On their own, they played more jazz than classical.

"Just for argument's sake," said Todd, "maybe Mr. G has a point about making a commitment."

Here we go again, thought Kyle, feeling the cheese go down like a golf ball. Todd's always wanted to get rid of me, maybe to go with just one trumpet or maybe because he wanted a clear shot at Nicole.

Everybody got quiet, suddenly into their pizza. Del started refilling glasses with Chianti. Kyle shook his head. He wanted another glass of wine, but he couldn't be less than sharp tomorrow on the roof. Kris would need his eyes up there. Kyle looked at the posters on Del's rec room walls, old-timey NASCAR stars—Junior Johnson, Richard Petty, Dale Earnhardt Sr., and Red Hoyt, who had been killed at Talladega in the same wreck in which Dad got hurt ten years ago. Hoyt had been a friend of Grandpa's.

Grandpa's poster was in the place of honor over the mantelpiece. He had signed it in his beautiful script: *Keep your eyes on the road ahead, Sir Walter Hildebrand, No. 12.* It was his famous slogan. People chanted it at him. *Keep your eyes on the road ahead.*

"Look." Todd wasn't done. "I'm not saying Mr. G was right, just that we all depend on each other here."

"Getting late," said Del. "You wanna play or bull-shit?"

"Kyle's got to think about his priorities," said Todd. My new number-one priority, thought Kyle, is to shove your trumpet down your throat.

"I saw that flick," said Jesse. "William Holden in *Golden Boy*. He had to choose between boxing and the violin."

"What did he choose?" asked Nicole, playing Jesse's straight man.

"I think he played between rounds," said Jesse, breaking himself up.

"I'm trying to make a point," said Todd.

"For argument's sake?" said Nicole sarcastically.

"C'mon," said Del. "Give Kyle a break. Family business."

"I saw that one, too," said Jesse. *The Godfather."*

"Okay, okay," said Todd. He switched gears and mimicked Mr. G. "Let's perpetrate some sound."

They played for another half hour, mostly Dizzy Gillespie, but they were lame. They quit before midnight. Del waved them out, said he would clean up. On the way Kyle said thanks to Del, who looked away. He would understand what I was going through, thought Kyle, but we've never gotten that close. Shy guy.

Outside, Todd said to Nicole, "Come on over, do some duets. I'll drive you home."

"Kyle's my ride," she said.

On the way back, Kyle slipped in a New York Trumpet Ensemble CD, as much to keep from talking as to break up the music in his head. Nicole popped it out. "Todd wasn't all wrong."

"So why you here?"

"Didn't feel like duetting him." She honked. "Want to come in? Nobody's home."

He felt warmth spreading downward. They'd started talking during the football marching band season when she'd first arrived in Goshen. Her parents were both new professors at the state college. Kyle had been hanging with her since the quintet got going again after football, but they hadn't taken the next step, becoming an official couple or even hooking up. "Got to be up at four thirty."

"I'll let you go home by then." He couldn't read her, never could. Was she teasing or being direct? Any other girl in school, he'd be hard and panting.

"Really got to go."

"Like what's the big deal tomorrow? It's your brother who's driving, right?"

"His regular spotter can't make the race." When he saw she didn't know what he was talking about, he said, "It's a team effort. Like the quintet."

"Whatever." She rolled her eyes. "Good luck tomorrow." The kiss was quick, but it was directly on his lips and felt real. A first. Maybe because she knew it wasn't going to lead anywhere. She grabbed her horn case and jumped out of the Camaro.

Driving back, he wondered why he hadn't gone in for a while. She was hot. Too hot? He wondered if he had enough experience for a New York girl. He liked her being different, but he wished she knew enough about racing to understand why he had to go.

When he pulled into his driveway, the house windows were wide open and Chopin poured out. When family was in the house or when she was demonstrating technique for her piano students, Mom played precisely, just enough energy to punch out the notes. When she thought she was alone, she let it rip, dropping notes all over the place but finding the romantic passion in the heart of the piece. Kind of typical, Kyle thought. Asses were tight in the Hildebrand family. The only place you were supposed to show emotion was on the track. The piano was her track.

The music spilling out of the house seemed to puddle around the Camaro, then flow up Hildebrand Hill, past Uncle Kale's house, dark except for the light in the bedroom where Aunt Susan was watching TV. Uncle Kale was probably in his motel room near Monroe Speedway right now, going over his notes and charts with Dad. Maybe even with Kris, if they had trapped him before he went out with Jackman and the boys.

The music streamed up toward the top of the hill and surrounded Grandpa Walter's big house, dark the night before a race except for the lights on the enormous wraparound porch.

Kyle remembered racing Kris on it around the house, by foot, on tricycles, scooters, bicycles, Rollerblades, skateboards, screaming as they bumped over loose slats and into each other, weaving around chairs, tables, gliders, dogs, people, watching the world around Hildebrand Hill whiz by, the dark Buckline Mountains stabbing a cloudless pale sky, then Lake Goshen shimmering blue, the green meadows dotted with Sir Walter's beef cattle and then the town itself, compact, white, boxy except for the church steeples and the control tower at the scrubby little airport alongside Goshen Raceway, new and gleaming in those days, and then the Buckline range again, a panoramic strip that reeled on and on until a grown-up made them stop or Kris, finally bored, hip-checked Kyle off the porch, down the stairs into Grandma Karen's flowers.

Grandma Karen had passed away and nobody was keeping up her flower beds. Goshen Raceway's grandstand was sagging and splintery and desperately needed a paint job. Grandpa would be in Monroe tonight with the new sponsors, charming them into spending enough millions to put Hildebrand Racing back in the big time.

Mom finished the Chopin and took a break. They

hadn't played together in a while. There wasn't that much music for trumpet and piano, but they sometimes managed to have fun improvising. Kyle waited until Mom was back at the piano again before he slipped out of the car. In the driveway lights he checked for oil under the car. Got to remember to stop for oil on the way to the track tomorrow. Better get over to the shop someday soon and fix the leak.

He tiptoed over the gravel until he was on grass. He let himself in the back door. The Labs, Rudy and Rozz, met him in the kitchen. He had to gently knee them away so he could get a soda out of the fridge and go upstairs.

There were new e-mails on his laptop. He wondered if Nicole was messaging him. She wrote a lot softer than she talked. Not going to read e-mail tonight. He kicked off his shoes and flopped on the bed. The dogs jumped up beside him. He laid his head on Rudy's flank. I'll rest a minute, he thought. Then maybe I'll check the e-mail. The faces on his wall, Miles and Dizzy and Wynton and Louis, and Philip Smith from when he came to play in Charlotte, were out of focus, like they were sleepy, too. They disappeared.

THREE

Just before he climbed into the car for the parade lap, Kris jerked his head at Kyle and winked, the old signal to haul your ass over here in a hurry, little brother. As usual, Kyle felt proud to be singled out and pissed off to be summoned like a dog. But he trotted over. It's a race day, he told himself, a Kris day. Keep your driver happy.

Kris grabbed Kyle's head and pulled him close. Even with Kris's mouth at his ear, Kyle barely heard him over the snarl and gunshots of dozens of engines warming up.

"Today," said Kris. "Gonna do it today."

"The sling?"

"Why don't you shout?"

"But Dad said . . ."

"Just be sure nobody's under me when I say 'Wilco.'"

17

He squeezed Kyle's head. "Wilco. Say it."

"Wilco." It was the name of a band Kris liked.

He loosened Kyle's head and turned it toward a crowd of people behind a barrier in the garage area. "Check the headlights on the redhead."

Big girl, almost as tall as they were, a fully packed Hildebrand Racing T-shirt and a number 12 baseball cap pulled low over her face. Couldn't make out her features. Her red hair was twisted into a braid that fell over one shoulder. Must be Kris's latest pit lizard. Kris cocked an index finger at the redhead, who cocked a finger back.

"What happened to the blonde?"

"Same old—she wanted a hand on the wheel." Kris released his head. "See you in Victory Lane. Don't forget. Wilco."

"Uncle Kale's gonna yank your tail in a knot."

"Not if I win." He pushed Kyle away. "Wilco."

Kris waved to fans screaming his name, his spiky black hair glistening in the sun. He was number three in the standings so far this season, his second in the Atlantic Division, and he'd won only two races, but the online polls had him listed as most popular, cutest, and most likely to be a NASCAR champion someday. Just like the Goshen High yearbook, thought Kyle. Kris brought his high school props to the track. Yeah, right, Kris'll listen to me.

Kris tapped fists with his pit crew captain, Jackman, a big ex-football player a few years older who followed Kris around like a tall dog, a one-man entourage. Kris was Jackman's ticket to the big time. He talked about being Kris's crew chief when he won his Nextel Cup championship in five years.

Whap! Kris slapped his gloved hands on the deep-blue roof of number 12. Crewmen from other cars stopped to watch him push up, then jackknife his body through the car window in a motion as smooth as an Olympic gymnast. Nobody else got into a car that way—too risky, you could fall on your can, smack your head, kick some piece of equipment. It was pure Kris Hildebrand, part Showtime, part psychological warfare. Coming up on dirt short tracks and regional series, he'd psyched out dozens of rivals with that maneuver before the race had even begun. It still gave Kyle a little shiver of pleasure and envy to watch that move.

"Better get upstairs." Uncle Kale's mouth was at his ear. Kyle hadn't seen him approach. "Keep your eyeballs peeled, Kylie. This ain't a music recital."

Suck my horn, Kyle thought. Uncle Kale had been giving him a hard time since he'd started missing races for the quintet. Uncle Kale had wanted Kyle on the pit crew, handling a tire, because Kris liked him around. Keep your driver happy.

"No daydreaming—keep your eyes peeled," said Uncle Kale.

Dad trudged up, his lanky body bent from the weight of his laptop and his loose-leaf binders. He limped. The burn scars on his legs still bothered him. He waited until Uncle Kale lumbered off before he said, "What'd Kris say?"

"About what?"

Dad's long face seemed to get longer. "The Family Brands people are sitting with Sir Walter, ready to sign. No time to goof around."

Kyle nodded.

"No banging, no wrecking, no stunts. Can I count on you?"

Like I'm my brother's keeper. "Do my best."

Dad nodded and trudged off. He'd spend the race in the pits at a table next to Uncle Kale, his oldest brother, watching the TV monitor as he kept his charts on gas consumption and tire wear. Has to be the worst job, Kyle thought. At least I'll be up high enough to breathe air I can't see.

Kyle walked across the racetrack, still smooth and cool, even as the day got hotter. Kyle liked this time just before the race, the sense of expectation, the stands chattery, the loudspeakers blaring country rock, the smell of cooking meat still stronger than the exhaust fumes. In just a few minutes the cars would be screaming over the track, grooving it, littering it with scraps of rubber, banging against each other as they jostled for position mile after mile after mile. Kris would be in the middle of the action, loving every lap. Kris once said he felt like he was inside a video game in mortal combat with thirty other killer studs. Kyle thought he had sounded high when he said it.

The white-haired guard who stood at the entrance to the iron spiral staircase that led up to the grandstand roof said, "Always been a fan of your family. I can get you on the VIP elevator."

"It's okay, thanks."

"Good race."

He preferred to climb, feeling the air change as he moved up, seeing the track spread out and grow smaller below him. The cars were circling the track now, around an infield jammed with thousands of people standing on top of their cars, trucks, trailers, motor homes. Some of them had camped out all week. The big NASCAR race would be tomorrow, when the grandstand would be packed with at least one hundred thousand spectators. Maybe only a quarter of that today. Only twenty-five thousand.

Maybe fifty people period at the Brooklyn Brass's master class. He'd rather be there.

Maybe three hundred at the Brass's 8 P.M. performance. He had his ticket in his wallet.

Missing the trumpet lesson with Mr. Sievers was bad enough, but master classes don't come around too often. Be a nice little trip. Maybe even stay over in Charlotte after the concert with Nicole.

Daydream about that later. Stay in the now. *Keep your eyes on the road ahead.*

From the roof of the grandstand, the cars lining up behind the pace car seemed no bigger than die-cast models. It almost seemed as though he could pick them up. They were only slightly less powerful than the mighty machines that raced in the multimillion-dollar NASCAR races.

Make it in the American Racing League and you had a clear shot at the big time.

He found the deep-blue number 12, nineteen cars back in the line of thirty-three. It should have placed higher in the qualifying runs, but the engine was overheating and they didn't want it to blow up. If they haven't fixed the problem, Kyle thought, we'll go home early, which is okay by me. I'll make the concert.

He remembered the sponsors sitting in a VIP suite with Sir Walter and felt guilty. The family needs to make this deal to get back into the major leagues.

He dug into his gym bag and fished out the radio and the big orange headphones. He dialed the team frequency. "Kyle here."

"Yo, little bro," said Kris. That was getting old. Got to tell him sometime. He listens to you, said Dad. Yeah, listens to me right into the flower bed.

"Kylie," said Uncle Kale. Getting tired of that baby name too. Nobody else called him Kylie. "Keep an eye on seventy-one and forty-two, desperate characters. You got that?"

"Copy."

"Look out for smoke," said Dad. He always said that. Mom once told Kyle that Dad was fire phobic. He had reason.

"Copy."

"Kylie." It was Uncle Kale again. "Which two numbers you keeping an eye on?"

He swallowed down the anger and the urge to say something smart-ass. When would Uncle Kale stop treating him like a kid? "Seventy-one and forty-two."

"You're awake," said Uncle Kale.

There were dozens of other spotters on the roof. He knew most of them by sight, but he hadn't been spotting enough the past couple of seasons to have made friends with any of them. Kris's regular spotter was an old guy,

Billy McCall, who had been Sir Walter's pit crew chief, his Jackman. Hope Billy passes those tests for his heart in Atlanta and gets back up here.

The racers formed into ranks of two abreast and followed the pace car around the half-mile track. Kris was twisting his wheel back and forth to keep his engine warm and to scuff his tires so they would grip better. As they circled, Kyle targeted the cars he'd be watching most closely.

Number 71 was Boyd Jurgensen, the only all-white car in the race, as white as Casper the Ghost because it didn't have a single sponsor logo on it. No kidding he was desperate to place high today. No sponsors, no money, no good engines, no testing, no spare parts. Boyd could get a lot of little sponsors if he wanted, but he was holding out for one big sponsor. Not a bad driver, but he was kind of an arrogant jerk who thought a lot of himself.

The yellow number 42 was Randall Bean, a nice old guy who owned his own car and had been around forever. He had raced against Sir Walter and he had raced against Kyle's dad. He was over fifty years old, but he couldn't let go the wheel, so he was driving down here in the minor leagues.

Keep an eye on number 24, Gary Nagle, Kris's biggest rival on the track among the younger drivers. He was twenty-three, four years older than Kris. His light-blue Chevy was a good car this season—he'd won the pole for this race.

Always got to watch the brick-red number 22, Ryan Ryder, as aggressive as Kris but without any of his finesse. Ryder was a bully. Kris would wreck you to win. Ryder would wreck you because you were there. The media had tagged him Ruff Ryder. He loved that.

The radio crackled and Kris yelled, "It's SHOW-time."

The green flag came down.

FOUR

Once the race began, Kyle swallowed down the resent-
ment he felt for being there. He liked the races, liked
figuring out the tactics of a hundred-mile-an-hour
chess match. He'd missed being part of it as a voice in
Kris's ear. His job wasn't to tell Kris what to do—
nobody told Kris what to do, although Dad and Uncle
Kale tried—but to give him information so he could
make the best decisions. And not too much information; like most crew chiefs, Uncle Kale wanted to keep
radio chatter at a minimum unless he himself had
something to say. But a spotter on the roof could see
things going on around the track that a driver or a
someone down in the pits couldn't see, a car moving up,
a car starting to smoke, a wreck unfolding.

In the early laps Kris slowly worked his way from nineteen to ten, picking off cars one at a time, coming up right behind them, intimidating them into getting out of his way or making a mistake that would let him pass. One of the big-time writers from Charlotte had called Kris The Intruder, even compared him to the great Dale Earnhardt Sr., who was The Intimidator.

Uncle Kale had warned Kris not to let his press clippings go to his head until he got to the Busch or Cup series and won a championship. Earnhardt had won seven. Kris had just grinned at that, and when Jackman had some "Intruder" caps made up, Kris made sure he wore one in front of Uncle Kale. Kris could get away with anything, always could.

Kyle checked the competition. Gary Nagle held his position in the lead. Ruff Ryder was three cars behind him. The desperate characters, Boyd Jurgensen in the ghostly white car and old Randall Bean, were in the back of the pack, nowhere near Kris. Number 73, a green Ford a few cars ahead of Kris, was driving aggressively, trying to bump cars out of his way. That was Elliott Slater, who used to race in the Busch series, just below the Cup. Slater was trying to make his comeback here. Keep an eye on him, too.

Kyle twisted his neck and stamped his feet to keep the blood moving. Stay sharp. It was still too early for the race to be interesting. Uncle Kale always said that there were drivers and there were racers, and a race didn't get interesting until the drivers had gotten out of the way of the racers. Kris was a racer. Sir Walter had been a racer back in the sixties and seventies, when number 12 was called the Blue Shadow for the way he stalked his prey before he passed them. Sir Walter was a cagey old fox. He was no Intimidator, not even an Intruder, but he could plot a race like a chess master, keeping his intentions a mystery until it was time to strike.

He was a lot more gentlemanly than Kris, on and off the track. He was always friendly and courteous and patient. Once a writer dubbed him Sir Walter, comparing him to a chivalrous knight. Kyle always had the feeling that Grandpa thought the name was too fancy. But it stuck, mostly because Grandpa's fans liked it. Dad thought it reminded them of Richard Petty, who was called King Richard. Kyle wondered if Grandpa liked the nickname. Never asked him. Of course, we never talk much.

Funny, Kyle thought, I usually think of him as Sir Walter, not Grandpa. Even Dad and Uncle Kale call him Sir Walter most of the time.

"You awake up there, Kylie?" said Uncle Kale.

No, I'm sleeping, lardass. "What's up?"

"Just checking."

Kris was holding his line nine cars behind Gary. The number 73 green Ford was running fifth, his rear end fishtailing toward the wall. Kyle wondered if Elliott Slater was having trouble controlling his car or just scaring people away. Something up with him, sneaky old pro.

Kyle wondered if Kris was serious about trying the sling today. Just like him to pull a risky stunt like that with the new sponsors watching. Then again, pull it off and they would be impressed. The Hildebrand Sling was a monster move.

The one time Grandpa had beat Richard Petty at Daytona, he had used the Hildebrand Sling, his most famous maneuver.

Late in a race, Sir Walter would come up on the leader, nose to tail, the Blue Shadow in stalk mode as the car in front weaved left and right to block him. Suddenly Sir Walter would swerve right, toward the outside wall, and if the other car responded to the move, he would swerve left and sling past him on the inside, his left-side wheels millimeters from going out of bounds on the grass.

Dad was pretty stubborn about Kris not trying the sling. All you needed would be someone coming up fast on either side and you could trigger the Big One, a twenty-car wreck. Dad was a lot more into safety than Uncle Kale, who was willing to let a driver take more risks to win. Of course, Uncle Kale had never been a driver and never been hurt badly, as Dad had been. And Kris didn't drive as carefully as Sir Walter had. Which was something else the family didn't talk about. A lot of people swore that Sir Walter with his talent would have whipped King Richard regularly if he had been willing to wreck, if he had a mean streak, the killer instinct.

Like Kris had.

It was a careful race, slow, averaging maybe eighty-five miles per hour. The cars were strung out single file. Kyle moved up to eighth place, then settled in again, awaiting his next intrusion. Kris was good at picking his moments, but he could use more patience. He'd get antsy after a while and make a move just to make a move. That's when he got into trouble. But he seemed okay now. There were plenty of laps to go. Kyle's mind began to drift. Even at this pace, as long as there weren't too many caution slowdowns or a major wreck, he might still get to Charlotte in time for the concert.

The radio crackled. Uncle Kale was talking to Kris. "How's she feel?"

"Twitchy," said Kris. "Wants to dust ass."

"Easy, you got lots of time," said Dad.

Uncle Kale said, "Kylie, check in if Ruff starts to move."

"That green Ford looks loose," said Kyle. "He's in fifth."

"Elliott Slater," said Dad. "He'll pull something if he can."

"Washed-up has-been," said Kris.

"Watch your mouth," said Uncle Kale, and the radio went off. Who knows who's listening in besides a few thousand fans with scanners?

The drivers had completed feeling each other out, like boxers in the early rounds. They had an idea now who had a strong car, who was bluffing, who was going to fade, who was playing possum until it was time to make a move.

Gary picked up the pace. He'd probably be pitting soon for gas and four tires, a good thing to do early, and he wanted as much lead as he could get. As expected, old Randall and Boyd in his naked white car had drifted to the rear of the pack.

Have to watch that, thought Kyle. Once they fell back far enough for Gary to come up behind them, you'd have two slow cars getting in the way. Old Randall was losing his reflexes and his car was waggling its butt. Boyd was an angry guy who would block Gary and Kris out of spite.

Ruff Ryder was making his move. He bumped a car out of his way and passed another.

Kyle tapped in. "Ryder's moved up behind Gary." He felt warm, dialed into the race. It's not so bad when you let yourself be part of it.

Kris picked off another car, then one more. He was now in sixth place in a front pack of nine. A couple of dozen strokers were strung out in the middle, then some cars lagging in the rear. A few cars were already in the pits with leaks and engine problems.

The stink of gas and toasted rubber was drifting up to the roof. Even with the orange headset on Kyle could hear the cars snarl and whine. Only up here it sounded like nasty cellos and violins fighting the bass thump of the crowd roar.

Randall and Boyd were a few minutes away from being lapped when Gary peeled off into the pits for gas and tires. Ruff followed him in. For some reason Uncle Kale wasn't calling Kris in, probably based on Dad's tire and gas calculations. It might be the worst job, but it won and lost a lot of races.

With the leaders in the pits, Kris was in third place now. Did Uncle Kale and Dad want him to take over the lead? Kris'd be the one to come up behind Randall and Boyd.

The crash began to unfold in Kyle's mind. He envisioned Randall and Boyd in the middle of the track as faster cars roared up. Kris's view would be blocked by the two cars ahead of him. They might escape by steering around, but Kris wouldn't have a chance as he slammed into Randall or Boyd and the cars behind him piled on.

A thought snagged the corner of his mind. Is this wishful thinking? A little wreck right now, just enough to disable number 12, nobody hurt, would get me out of here. Make the concert.

Might even make some of the master class.

He felt nauseous and swallowed the thought, but it came right back up like the acid orange juice. A wreck that took Kris out of action for a little while, at least till Billy's back spotting, would let him get back to the quintet.

How can you think like that?

Well, as long as I keep trotting up like a dog whenever Kris calls me, as long as I say, "What time?" whenever Kris needs a tire changer, Kris needs a spotter, the family needs a second man in the hauler, I'm going to be living Kris's life, not my own. Kyle thought he had broken free when Mom convinced Dad to let him stop racing during band season his sophomore year. Fat chance of being free in this family.

Keep your eyes on the road ahead.

The two cars in front of Kris took the third turn and headed into the straightaway, arrows aimed at Randall and Boyd, who were squatting like roadkill in the middle of the track. They had plenty of time to drive around them. Kris's view would be blocked until it was too late.

Kyle said, "Drop back, Kris, you're clear high."

In Kyle's mind the toy cars slowed so he could reach down and rearrange them. His mind touched the Blue Shadow.

He could almost feel Kris twist the wheel right and point the car toward the wall, the high side, spinning and slowing once there was no one ahead or behind. Sparks flew as he rubbed the wall, but he kept control and steered around Randall and Boyd.

"Thanks, little bro." He sounded like he meant it.

Kyle was jacked. For a moment there he had felt inside the car, and that felt good.

Gary and Ruff came out of the pits and worked their way back near the front. Kris had taken the lead. The race had settled into a battle for split seconds. The over-the-wall guys would be busting butts to get their cars in and out of the pit in less than fifteen seconds, and the crew chiefs would be plotting tactics for the final laps, especially when to try to move to the front.

Kyle could make out Dad hunched over his laptop and charts at a table overlooking the number 12 pit, could imagine him lost in his gas and tire calculations. A good or bad decision about when to fill up the tank or how many tires to change could make all the difference in a race this close.

Nobody was making any risky moves yet. Kyle

struggled to keep his mind from drifting from the race to the quintet, then let it split-screen. He could think about both.

He was sorry to be missing the master class; it could be awesome, a chance to watch serious musicians up close, to learn and be inspired. The Brooklyn Brass was one of the best ensembles in the country. Their two trumpets also played in symphony orchestras and did jazz gigs. He had their CDs. Getting some pointers from a group like that, he thought, could get us tighter, move us toward our own sound. Some group—we don't even have a name.

Mom is the only one in the family who understands what the quintet means, he thought. She was the only other musician in the family. But she almost always came down on the family side when there was a conflict. Like every other Hildebrand. I should talk. I'm here today, right?

The radio crackled. "Pit now, Kris."

"I'm good," said Kris. He didn't want to give up the lead.

"Not enough gas," said Dad.

Kris slowed into the pit road as Gary and Ruff swept to the lead. Kyle turned back to number 12 just in time to see Kris's gasman drop his seventy-pound dump can. The rear tire handler tripped over it. It would have been worse if he'd fallen down, but Jackman leaned over and caught him with one powerful hand. At least ten precious seconds were lost. Uncle Kale was cursing as Kris drove back onto the track.

Kris needed almost twenty laps to work his way back up to the front, ten miles that tested his patience, which Kyle thought was wearing thin. The Intruder was moving cars out of his way, one of them into the wall and out of the race. Kris knew how to make enemies.

With twenty laps to go, Kris got up to fourth place. He stayed there as the bright, hard sun of the afternoon began to weaken, changing the temperature of the track. Cars began to push toward the wall as the grip of the track tightened. Kyle could feel the suspense building in the crowd. When would Kris make his move?

He waited until there were only five laps to go.

The crowd was on its feet, yelling, as Kris tried to break the three-car jam in front of him. Gary, Ruff, and Elliott Slater were running side by side, but Slater in the green Ford was waggling his back end again. He didn't have full control of the car.

Kyle imagined himself in Kris's seat, the heat building up inside his fire suit, his arms aching from turning the wheel, his eyes burning from staring through the oil-spattered windshield, his head pounding from the carbon monoxide buildup. He thought he could feel the thumping in Kris's chest as the lap counter on the scoreboard clicked down.

He thought, Do you want to be in that seat, li'l bro?

Just imagining, so I can help Kris.

Whatever you say.

Minutes to go before the finish line and three cars in front. Going to have to do something soon.

The radio crackled. "Talk to me, Kyle."

"Green Ford's loose, he's gonna have to drop back."

"Oh, yeah." He could hear the anticipation in Kris's voice, and then, "There he goes," as Slater slowed the green Ford to get it back under control.

The green Ford was running alongside Kris. There were only two cars in front of him now. Ruff shot ahead to take the lead.

Kris accelerated into Gary's rear end. It looked like Kris was sticking his nose up Gary, bumping him on the straightaway. But Gary kept up enough speed so Kris couldn't knock him out of the way. And there was no way Gary would let him pass, smoothly blocking as Kris edged left and then right. Gary's good, thought Kyle.

The radio crackled. "Wilco," said Kris.

Kyle had forgotten.

The Hildebrand Sling.

"What?" That was Dad and Uncle Kale at the same time.

"Talk to me, Kyle," shouted Kris.

"No," said Kyle.

"What's up?" Dad must know, thought Kyle.

"Wilco," snarled Kris.

He's going to do it with or without me, thought Kyle.

Kyle felt his mind slip into the zone, the toy cars slowing so he could reach down and touch them. Ruff's brick-red number 22 was in front, Gary's light-blue number 24 right behind him, and then Kris running alongside Slater's green Ford. Kris was on the inside, Slater on his right, on the outside near the wall.

"Clear low." Kyle concentrated all his mental energy on number 12.

Kyle's arms tensed as if he were jacking the wheel on the Blue Shadow himself, swerving right in a feint that banged the green Ford up toward the wall and out of the action. Gary edged right to block Kris.

Kyle yelled, "Sling!"

Kyle's arms throbbed as he imagined Kris yanking the wheel left, a vicious twist that made the Blue Shadow's chassis shiver and shriek. The car swooped low, the left-side wheels almost touching the grass.

It was like threading a needle. Gary recovered and turned left, and Slater came roaring up alongside him.

There shouldn't have been enough room for Kris to pass, but somehow he slipped through, passing Gary, then passing Ruff.

Kris crossed the finish line first.

As the checkered flag came down, the green Ford caught up with number 12 and slammed into its rear. Son of a bitch. Slater didn't have to do that, thought Kyle. The race was over.

The crowd gasped as the Blue Shadow lurched forward, rose up on its rear wheels like a Jurassic Park monster with a shriek of wounded metal, then fell sideways. It rolled over on its roof, now a helpless blue turtle.

Kyle was frozen until Kris crawled out his window, stood up, and swaggered around his car, waving. The crowd went wild.

SIX

The girl with the red braid was even better-looking up close. She was about eighteen or nineteen. Her skin was milky white except for tan freckles splashed across the bridge of her nose and high on her cheeks. Round brown eyes, a wide friendly mouth with lots of big white teeth. Kris could pick 'em.

"You must be Kyle," she said. "You look just like Kris except for the hair."

That stopped him. She grabbed his arm as he was holding up his pass to the guard at the entrance to Victory Lane. He noticed that the pass around her neck wouldn't get her in.

"He should let his hair grow long like yours," she said.

The guard checked Kyle's pass and waved them both through. Cool maneuver, he thought, impressed and annoyed at the same time. She used me to get to Kris. "Who are you?" It came out more harshly than he intended.

"Jimmie," she said, and let go his arm to push her way into the crowd around the Blue Shadow, which had been turned back on its tires.

Kris was dancing on the dented roof of the car, spurting soda down on Jackman and the crew. The champagne would come later, Kyle thought. With Jimmie.

Kris spotted him and gave him the wink and the head jerk before he jumped down from the car. He seemed a little shaky when he landed, but Jackman steadied him. Jimmie gave Kris a hug. Dad and Uncle Kale were nearby, gassing with Sir Walter and some men in suits. Must be the Family Brands guys. The way everyone was grinning, thought Kyle, it must be a done deal.

Kris was talking into a mic, thanking everyone, while Jackman handed him different pit caps to clap on his head so pictures could be taken with each of the sponsors' logos. The old hat dance. Lots of little sponsors. That might be changing.

Kyle suddenly felt lonely. What's wrong with me? Kris won and I was part of it. Get with the team, man. But what does this have to do with me? It's not where I want to be. He watched the crew, hopping up and down like kids, so happy to win, especially after they nearly blew it dropping the gas can.

"Kyle." Kris was waving him over. "KYLE!"

Did enough for you today—I don't have to join the crowd kissing your ass. He turned away. Rather sit in my car in the traffic inching out of the speedway than stand around here like a fifth wheel.

A big hand dropped on his shoulder and spun him around. "Hey, Kyle, go get your props." Jackman was grinning. "Man, you deserve it. Wilco. Wouldn't be here without you."

"Later." He tried to get away, but Jackman was too strong.

"Kris wants you." He steered Kyle to the car.

Kris let go of the redhead and grabbed Kyle. He still had the mic. "And here's the man steered me across the line, my baby brother Kyle."

The suits and Sir Walter started clapping, but they were quickly drowned out by Jackman and the crew stomping and yelling. Kris poured soda on Kyle's head.

It felt great. He couldn't keep himself from smiling. He didn't even mind when Jimmie hugged him. The photographers moved closer.

Sir Walter glided over and took the mic from Kris. His silvery hair was long and carefully combed, his blue eyes twinkled. He looked like a movie actor playing an old-time race car driver. His deep, rumbly voice sounded like Johnny Cash over the public address system. "Watching my grandson win today was a bigger thrill than winning myself, maybe 'cause he's better'n I was his age." He paused to shake his head and grin at fans yelling, "No way, Sir Walter," from the grandstand. "Well, the folks at Family Brands must've thought so, too, 'cause they're gonna partner Hildebrand Racing. Next week number twelve will be wearing a new paint job and a new logo. So you show them our appreciation by buying up Jump and Yum Cakes and Fresh Beginnings cereal. Just tell 'em at the store that Sir Walter sent you."

Sir Walter put on his modest face as the crowd shouted, "Keep your eyes on the road ahead." The Family Branders were high-fiving one another. What a bunch of jerks, thought Kyle. Another reason to be glad I'm not on the inside of this deal.

A track official signaled to Kris. "Docs are waiting for you." He'd need the usual medical exam after a crash.

"Right there." Kris grabbed Kyle's head and pulled it to his mouth. "Gonna stay over. Need your car."

"How'm I gonna get home?"

"Fly back with grandpa in the money boys' jet. They saved a seat for me."

44

"Sure it's okay?"

"C'mon. For ten million bucks don't you think they want to keep their driver happy? Keys."

Kyle dug out his car keys. Kris grabbed them and was gone. Kyle didn't have time to tell Kris about the Camaro's oil leak. Kris said something to Sir Walter, who nodded and said something to one of the men in suits, who came over and steered Kyle toward a golf cart that would take him to the Monroe Speedway airfield. Wheels up in twenty minutes, said the suit.

SEVEN

The airplane seat was so soft, Kyle would have fallen asleep if he'd been more relaxed around Sir Walter and the Family Brands guys. He'd never been totally comfortable with his grandfather, who always seemed to care as much about his fans as his family. He was always super friendly around fans, always willing to stop and chat, even sign autographs in the middle of dinner at a restaurant. Especially in the middle of dinner with his family, where he never had much to say.

Sir Walter didn't start talking with Kris and Kyle until they were old enough to talk racing. Sir Walter and Uncle Kale were the only adults in the family who thought the two little brothers racing around the enormous porch was funny. Of course, when the inevitable end came, when Kyle went flying into the flowers, Sir Walter and Uncle Kale were never around to pick him up.

When Kris was sixteen, before his first big televised race, Sir Walter gave him two pieces of advice.

"You got to establish your territory and hold it," he said, and then, "Always have a spare Sharpie so no fan walks away disappointed because they didn't get an autograph."

Kris laughed when he told Kyle about the advice, which he thought was dumb. Kyle laughed because Kris laughed, but it didn't sound dumb to him. He had wondered when Sir Walter would tell it to him. It had never happened. It would never happen now, he thought. I'm a trumpet player, not a racer. Not even a trumpet player today.

A flight attendant took drink orders. Kyle looked around. There were about a dozen people on the plane, mostly older men in lounge chairs fiddling with their BlackBerrys. Sir Walter was sitting at a table in the rear, going over papers with two of the suits. Must be the contracts. Dad always said Sir Walter was as good with sponsors as he'd been behind the wheel.

"This is just the small jet, for short hops." A bald, chubby suit was leaning toward him from the next chair. He extended a hand. "I'm Dave Winik, vice president of communications for Family Brands."

"I'm Kyle . . ."

"I know you, the super spotter." Winik grinned. "So what's this sling thing I heard about?"

The flight attendant stepped between them. Winik was very fussy about his drink order, some kind of martini that sounded like pure gin. Wouldn't mind a beer myself, Kyle thought, but better not here.

"You want a drink?" Winik raised his eyebrows. "I won't tell anyone."

Kyle decided to outcool him. "I'll have Jump."

Winik made a face. "I only have it with rum, call it Rump." Funny story to tell Nicole. Wonder what she's doing tonight after the concert. "You race too, right?"

"Used to."

"What happened?" He pushed his face up close, looked serious, like a guidance counselor.

"Got into music." It was enough for this guy.

"Oh, yeah? What do you play?" He had a notebook out.

"Trumpet."

Winik wrote that down. "Your brother's the designated driver, huh?" He laughed at his little joke. He wrote that down too. Kyle wished the plane would land already. "All these Ks in the family—Kris, Kyle, Kale, Kerry, that's your dad, right?"

"That was my grandpa's idea. For Grandma Karen."

"That's great stuff." He chuckled and wrote it down.

"There was a Ken, too. Your dad's other brother?"

"He's in the army," said Kyle. The one who got away, Mom called him. Winik didn't need to know that.

The flight attendant came back with their drinks. Winik tasted his martini and shrugged. Kyle took a gulp of the Jump because he was thirsty. Worst of the sports drinks.

The plane landed before either of them finished their drinks. Winik made a phone call. "Your limo's on the way. See you tomorrow."

"Tomorrow?"

"We're doing a little event at the church. Get some footage for the marketing campaign."

The limo was waiting at the foot of the stairway. Too bad he couldn't ask the driver to take him to the concert in Charlotte.

The limo was just for him and Sir Walter. He tried to remember when he'd last been alone with his grandfather. Maybe never. He worried about what they would talk about, then felt more put out than relieved when Sir Walter started talking with the driver. Another fan.

They were near Goshen when Sir Walter turned to him and said, "I heard it was you called for the sling."

Not quite, he thought, but he didn't know how much

credit to take to keep Kris out of trouble. Hey, how can Kris get into trouble for the win that clinched the big deal? It turned out he didn't need to answer, because it wasn't really a question.

"Good call. Fred would of gotten a boot out of that, rest his soul. Y'know, it was your Great-grandpa Fred invented the sling right before Bristol one year, to beat Bobby Allison, and it worked perfect, like today. Beat King Richard, too, at Daytona. You gotta know when to call 'em, and you sure did. You feel good about that call, Kyle. We got a deal, and I think the family's back on track."

Kyle felt breathless. He didn't want the ride to end. He wanted to say something, but his grandfather turned back into Sir Walter and leaned forward to pick up his conversation with the driver. They talked about old-time races until they arrived at Hildebrand Hill. Kyle was let out first, and Sir Walter gave him a little pat-on-the-shoulder good night.

EIGHT

As usual Kyle slept through most of church with his eyes open. It was a gift, the one thing of his Kris envied. Kris needed to wear dark glasses to sleep through church, on the rare occasions he showed up anymore. Kyle wondered where he was, on the road beating the hell out of the old Camaro that had once been his or just waking up in a motel room with the redhead. He wondered why he should care, then slipped into a dozy half sleep. The heavy-handed organ music felt like a blanket.

Before he could get all the way under, Dad jabbed an elbow into his ribs. Pastor Mike must be talking about us. A camera crew was kneeling in a corner, cutting back and forth between the pastor and the

Hildebrands in the front pew.

"How many times have I said that prayers don't weigh you down, they give you downforce? Well, your prayers worked yesterday. I know Kris Hildebrand's win was a result of his own skill and daring and faith, but I believe he never would have gotten to the finish line without that unseen hand that guides us all. Yesterday that unseen hand swept him past three other cars on the last turn of the last lap. Thank the Lord. The Hildebrands are with us today, and they've brought some friends from Family Brands, the fine folks who make Yum Cakes and Jump and all those great cereals we love in God's good morning. Make them welcome. They've got a little treat for you after the service."

Kyle kept a smile on his face until the camera turned back to Pastor Mike. Kyle noticed Grandpa's face was frozen in its usual Sir Walter smile. Wonder if he sleeps with his eyes open too. Can't imagine having that discussion. But after last night's big breakthrough in the limo, who knows? That is so pathetic, considering that little chat a breakthrough with your own grandfather. Mom's dad had died before Kyle got to know him. We hardly see her side of the family. Too far away. They're a lot looser than Hildebrands—you can talk to them.

He felt jangly after the service. He usually came out of church feeling mellow, but now he felt like marching up to Pastor Mike and saying, "Want to shake the unseen hand?" What's your problem, Kylie?

Outside the church, Dad muttered, "Kris should be here," and Kyle said, "Probably got back too late after the medical exam. And the crash inquiry." Why am I always covering for him?

"I was there, took all of five minutes." He lowered his voice. "We got to talk."

"What about?"

"The sling." He looked more hurt than angry. "Without telling me?"

"It worked."

"That's not the point."

Kyle thought, What is the point?, but before he could think of something to say, Pastor Mike pushed between them and grabbed Kyle's hand. "Hope to see you at Youth Group, Kyle. We're planning a musical evening."

Kyle nodded. Before he had to come up with something noncommittal, Pastor Mike turned to give Sir Walter a double-handed pump and then shake with the Family Brands suits. One of them was the chubby note-taker, Winik, who gave Kyle a big smile and wave, like they were buds. The camera crew was walking backward, shooting everything. In the church parking lot tables were piled with paper shopping bags covered with the Family Brands green-and-red logo. He wondered how that logo was going to look on Hildebrand deep blue.

Mom grabbed his arm and whispered, "How's the unseen hand?"

It smoothed a little of the morning's rough edge knowing she was still on his side. "Dad's ticked off."

"And he's right. It was dangerous."

Dad caught up with them. "What are you guys plotting?"

"Slinging out of here," said Mom.

"Not funny, Lynda."

They watched the congregation swarm around the paper bags. They were filled with Family Brands food and drinks.

Mom said, "Famine relief comes to Goshen."

"C'mon, Lynda," said Dad. "It's a good thing."

"I hope so."

Kyle felt edgy and sour. He'd tried to get Nicole, by cell phone and IM, but there was no answer. He imagined her spending the night in Charlotte with Todd. Or maybe even with Mr. G, who was married but liked to look down girls' halter tops.

"Hey, Kylie." Uncle Kale lumbered over. "You ever try something like that again, I'm gonna stuff that trumpet where your brains are."

"Kris won."

"Only reason I'm not doing it."

Kyle watched him lumber off. Always hard to believe he and Dad were brothers, long, thin Dad so calm and kindly, humongous Kale always angry and know-it-all. People said Kale was a genius in the garage, he could put his ear on a car's hood and diagnose what was wrong with the engine, but he could be such an asshole. Kris said Uncle Kale never got over wanting to be a driver instead of a crew chief, but Sir Walter had spotted his mechanical ability early and made the decision for him. Besides, he was too fat to squeeze into a car.

Winik bustled up. "Where's Kris?"

Not my brother's keeper. "He know about this?"

"He promised to be here when I gave him my hotel key." Winik glanced at his watch. "Camera crew's got a plane to catch."

So Kris had slept over in Winik's hotel room with the redheaded girl. Why is she stuck in my mind? Sir Walter strolled by, his arms around Pastor Mike and the organist. Winik signaled the camera crew to shoot them.

"This going to be in a commercial?" said Kyle.

"Certainly in a sales presentation," said Winik. "Hildebrand is a Family Brand. That's the new slogan. What do you think?"

It stinks. Kyle said, "Catchy."

"There's our boy," said Winik, pointing.

Kris was pale and wobbly. His smile looked pasted on. Jackman's shoulder was against his, supporting him and moving him along like a sheepdog. The big crew captain was almost always by Kris's side, ready to play with him or fight for him, but today he looked prepared to catch him. Must have been some night with the redhead, Kyle thought, until he remembered the crash at the end of the race and felt a splash of fear. You never can tell about those crashes. Head injuries.

The video crew surrounded Kris and herded him to the tables, where he hugged and high-fived his way through the congregation. Kris always knew what to do. He shook hands with Pastor Mike, threw an arm over Sir Walter's shoulder, slapped palms with Dad, and hugged Mom. The camera recorded every move.

Jackman steered Kris through the crowd and into the back entrance of the church. Just before he closed the door behind them, Jackman called out, "Kyle!"

By the time Kyle was inside the church, Kris was on his knees in the bathroom, vomiting.

Jackman looked worried. "All morning."

Kris wiped his mouth with his sleeve. "Some bad pepperoni—it's all out now. Listen, Kyle, you got a leak. Bad pan gasket, for one thing. The car's in the garage now. . . ."

He fainted.

NINE

The doctor came out of the examining room in golf clothes. "X-rays of Kris's head showed nothing." When nobody else smiled, he added, "Old joke. A mild concussion. We'll do an MRI if symptoms persist."

"Such as?" asked Mom.

"Memory loss, dizziness, extreme fatigue . . ."

"He can drive next week," said Dad. It sounded to Kyle like a statement, not a question.

"Tell you in a couple of days," said the doctor.

"Need to know before that."

"Do the best I can, Kerry. What did the track doctors say?"

"Those quacks," said Kris, buttoning his shirt as he came out of the examining room.

"What did they say?"

Kris was avoiding the question. "Just got my bell rung, is all. Happened all the time in football."

"Why we made you quit football," said Mom. "You had two concussions, remember?"

The doctor said, "What did you feel on impact?"

"Don't even remember crossing the finish line."

"Really?" The doctor frowned. "Call me tomorrow morning, Kerry. We'll keep a close eye on this."

"You're coming home with us, Kris," said Mom.

Kyle expected Kris to object, but he just shrugged. "Anything to make you happy, Mom."

Kyle hitched a ride to the garage with Jackman, who kept shaking his head. "I should've just taken him to the ER in Monroe this morning. He didn't look right."

"Maybe he had a rough night with the redhead." Where did that come from?

Jackman shot him a glance. "He got to the hotel and went to sleep. By himself. Now that shoulda told me something right there."

There were a dozen cars in the parking lot behind the Hildebrand Racing garage. The glass-and-stone build- ing rose three stories high, a football field wide. When Fred and Sir Walter built it, only Dale Earnhardt's garage was bigger. Kris and Kyle had grown up playing in the gift shop and the museum, chatting with fans, and then working in the repair bays and the fabrication rooms. Kyle had even practiced his trumpet in a back room until Uncle Kale complained that it was drowning out engine sounds. Once Kyle stopped racing, he never hung out when he didn't have to. Kris was here all the time, talking to the mechanics and the engine builders. For Kyle spending three weeks at music camp last summer had felt like an escape.

Jackman unlocked a back door. Kyle heard the clang of barbells from the gym. Jackman had called a rare Sunday crew meeting to screen the video of their pit stops and to work out. The screwup with the gas can could have cost Kris the race. Jackman went into the weight room.

Kyle spotted his Camaro in a repair bay, on a lift. The redhead was peering up at it. Her braid was tucked inside a cap. When she saw him, she said, "Don't you ever listen to your car? You drive like Kris."

It was no compliment the way she spat it out. He felt off-balance and blurted, "What are you doing here?"

"Drove your car back. Kris rode home with Jeff."

It took him a moment to remember Jackman's name was Jeff Myers. He'd been calling himself Jackman for years, ever since he had talked Uncle Kale into letting him take over the top spot on the pit crew. "Well, thanks. You going to fix it or just take it apart?"

"I can fix it." She sounded insulted. "I'm a certified mechanic, and I've crewed in modified and late model. Drove 'em, too. What?"

"I didn't say anything."

"You don't believe me?" She waved a wrench in an oily hand. "You thought I was some groupie?"

"No offense—I didn't think about you at all." He liked the way that rocked her back, but she recovered, nodded, and turned again to the underside of the Camaro.

"When's it gonna be ready?"

"When I fix what you broke."

He walked away. Three bays down, Dad was circling number 12. The car was scraped and dented. The back panels were smashed in where the green Ford had rear-ended it at the finish. "Took some shot there."

"You know Slater?" said Kyle.

"He ran Busch and Craftsmen Truck, did okay, woulda gone up to the Cup series, but he couldn't get along with anybody. He's trying to restart his career."

"Some start. He should get set down for that."

Dad shrugged. "Hard to prove it was deliberate." He took a breath. "You kind of leave yourself real vulnerable with the sling."

"Wouldn't've won otherwise."

"True. When you boys cook that up?"

Never lie to Dad. "Just before the race."

He nodded. "Kris been practicing it?"

"Not that I know."

"Kale's pretty wound up. If Kris misses any races, he's gonna chew your ear."

"Did already."

"That's his way." He put his hand on Kyle's shoulder. "I know you thought you were doing the right thing."

That made Kyle feel worse. Kris better be okay. For me as well as for him.

TEN

He thought he'd be glad to have Kris home even though he didn't expect a return to the days before he had moved into a condo in town with Jackman last year. Back then Kris'd invite Kyle into his room for video games, TV football, a wrestling match. At the very least Kyle figured he'd have someone to talk to who wouldn't be laying on a guilt trip for calling the sling or missing the Brooklyn Brass in Charlotte.

But he hardly saw Kris even though he was next door in his old bedroom. Meanwhile, Mr. G and the other brass players didn't give him a hard time. They weren't angry or disappointed that he had missed Charlotte; they just felt sorry for him. The trip had energized them, brought them closer as an ensemble, and left him out. When they played, he felt he was missing signals. On breaks they reminisced about the trip, discussed techniques they'd picked up. They didn't try to include him. Were they punishing him? Did they think he wanted to bail on them? He avoided Nicole, who didn't seem to notice.

His makeup lesson with Mr. Sievers was a little tense. He had barely practiced the new piece. Mr. Sievers already thought he was giving Mr. G and the quintet too much time.

Kris was asleep when Kyle left for school and at the garage when he got back. The family didn't eat together until Tuesday night. Kris looked tired. He picked at Mom's lamb shanks, usually a holiday meal and one of his favorites. Dad frowned through dinner, something on his mind. Mom didn't try to get a conversation going. The silence was so uncomfortable, they were glad when Uncle Kale dropped in for dessert. He was a lot nicer in the house than in the shop.

"Brought your beast back, Kylie. Runs sweet."

It took him a moment to remember the Camaro had been in the shop. He'd been driving one of the pickups to school. "Thanks."

"That girl's a wrench, let me tell you. She was working the NASCAR Dodge series before she came here. Gonna let her temp in the shop." There was no edge in his voice. Uncle Kale was up to something. He shoveled down Mom's cobbler. "Top of your game, Lyn." He stood up. "Gotta go feed the dogs. Susan's got a meeting tonight." Aunt Susan ran Hildebrand Construction along with a haircutter franchise. Uncle Kale was at the door when he turned and said casually, "Gonna want you around next weekend, Kylie."

Kyle looked around the table. Mom was looking down, and Dad was nodding at him. A group decision, but they let Uncle Kale deliver the message. Made it official business, not a request from Dad.

"How come?"

"Just in case," said Uncle Kale.

Just in case of what? thought Kyle, but he was already thinking ahead to an answer. Billy can't make it. Changes in the pit crew. Backup driver for Kris. That one stuck in his throat. No way.

Uncle Kale was out the door and Dad was turning on the Speed Channel. End of discussion.

Kyle gave homework a run but couldn't stay with it. No interesting e-mail. He realized that most of his friends were in the band, especially in the quintet. He tried to practice the trumpet, but his mouth stayed dry.

The bass line of country music slapped against the wall he shared with Kris. It was the music Kris played when he was down. It was also a signal to come on in.

He'd pull a bottle of Makers Mark from under the bed.

Kris was sprawled in the ratty old leather lounger they had salvaged years ago from one of Grandma Karen's spring cleaning binges. He barely looked up. "What part of knocking's too hard for you?"

"Hitting the door 'stead of you." An old routine that almost got a smile out of him. "Wassup?"

"Siddown." Kris waited until Kyle had plopped down on his bed. The room was exactly as he had left it a year ago, trophies and video games everywhere. Kris pointed under the bed and nodded as Kyle found the bottle and pretended to take a big pull. He liked the sharing ritual more than the taste. He held the bottle out to Kris, who shook his head. "My head's loose."

"What the doctors say?"

"They don't know diddley. I'm taking pills." He thumbed the remote to lower the volume, and whispered. "Kyle, I'm seeing double."

"You tell anybody?"

"You kidding?"

"You gonna race?"

"Wait and see."

"How long?"

"Dad could replace me last minute. Don't give me that look—you haven't been in the garage last two days. Sponsors all over the place, fabricators on overtime, painters, even a gay tailor from Hollywood making the fire suit. You imagine if I said I was seeing double? Family Brands can still back out."

"Be better than seeing double in a race."

Kris's laugh had a nasty edge. "No problem. Instead of thirty cars, you drive against sixty."

ELEVEN

At practice on Wednesday Mr. G was floating out of his plaid pants. "You are not . . . going . . . to believe this."

Todd whispered, "He got laid."

Jesse farted and Nicole honked.

"We have been invited to perform with the Brooklyn next fall." He whooped. Jesse and Del bumped fists. Nicole and Todd hugged. Kyle just sat there, imagining the quintet shrinking into a quartet.

"This is truly amazing. I just got an e from Terence himself." He paused to let everyone nod at that. "A major grant came through—Brooklyn Brass will be the ensemble in residence at the arts center. They will tour middle schools. There will be a slot for a high school group. They want us." He suppressed a squeal. "It's pro forma, but state rules require an audition, so, people, we need to prepare a classical piece, a marching piece, and a jazz piece. We have four weeks. Can we do it?"

It took Kyle a moment to realize that Mr. G was staring at him. He nodded. Everyone else was squawking notes.

"Also, we are going to need a name. Next Monday I want every one of us, myself included, to come in with three names. I hear yes?"

He was still staring at Kyle. This time he blew off a squawk too. He felt bogus.

After practice Nicole caught up with him in the parking lot. Her hair was pulled back from her face. She is pretty, he thought. "Don't you talk to me anymore?"

"About what?" said Kyle.

"Don't you want to be part of this Brooklyn thing?"

"Was I voted out or something?"

"Are you paranoid?"

"What's your point?"

She snorted. "Don't blow it. You're better than Todd. Mr. G thinks so too, but he's going to have to pick a first trumpet, at least for the jazz piece. You gotta show some enthusiasm."

He wondered if Mr. G had really said he was better than Todd. He wasn't sure he was. "I'm here. I couldn't help last Saturday."

"How about next Saturday? We could work on names."

"Gotta go to the race."

"How long's this gonna go on?"

There was too much to explain. "Till it's over."

"That's all you got to say?" She waited a beat for an answer, then pivoted on one black boot and marched away. He thought of Uncle Kale leaving after ordering him to show up next weekend. Nobody wants to hear from me.

What is it I want to say?

He drove to the garage. The Camaro purred all the way. It had never sounded so happy. Jimmie had replaced the shocks and springs, too.

Kris was in the main office, standing on a box while two men in tight, shiny white T-shirts circled him, murmuring to each other through the pins in their mouths. Kris was wearing the new Family Brands uniform, shifting from foot to foot.

"What do you think, Kyle?" It was Winik, the pudgy suit who had asked him questions in the plane.

"Looks good." It was ugly. The Family Brands red-and-green logo clashed with the Hildebrand deep blue.

Kris rolled his eyes at Kyle. They were bloodshot. "How much longer? I got to sit in the car, see if that fits, too."

One of the tailors said, "We do need to get this right."

"My brother's the same size, how about you use him as a model?"

The tailors looked Kyle over, then shrugged at each other. One of them said, "Be careful getting out of the suit—the pins."

The suit fit fine. Felt good, snug in the right places, just enough room in the seat. He could always wear Kris's clothes, because he'd always been bigger for his age than Kris had been. Dad came by while Kyle was standing on the box and thanked him. "We needed Kris in the car." Dad was smiling. "No more one size fits all."

The Family Brands money meant that the car would be tailored not only to Kris's size but his driving style: heavier brakes for his tendency to ride them coming into the turns, more plating on the right side because he rubbed the wall a lot. Kyle wondered if the car would fit him, too, like the uniform. Why am I thinking this?

"Looks good," said one of the tailors. "You twins?"

"Kris is almost two years older."

"You stand quieter."

When they were finished, Kyle wandered into the shop. Kris was in the new car. At the moment it was more of a gray metal wrap than a car. A dozen men stood around nodding and muttering, measuring and making notations. It was a part of racing Kyle had never gotten into. The real gearheads could get off on a shock valve. At music camp there were counselors who creamed over trumpet valves. But this was more than that. Hildebrand Racing hadn't had the money to build exactly what it wanted since the days when Sir Walter was still racing and Dad was a hot young gun. Back then they even raced a third car sometimes. Then Sir Walter retired and Dad got hurt and the business slumped, just getting by on endorsements and T-shirt sales and Uncle Kale and Dad working part-time for other teams. Up until now Kris's cars were hand-me-downs. Now they would be made-to-order, and there would be backups.

"Pretty exciting, huh?" said Winik. "At the creation."

"Not enough time for testing," said the redheaded girl, joining them.

Who asked you, Kyle thought, then took a breath. "Hey, thanks for fixing the Beast. Never ran so good."

"You could keep it that way," she said. "Change your oil before it turns to mud."

"Yes, sir," said Kyle. He was getting annoyed again.

"Excuse me," said Jimmie. "I'm working on a car."

Winik watched her walk away. There was a swing to her tail. "Who's that?"

Some pit bunny trying to weasel her way in. Kyle said, "A part-time mechanic."

"You know, Family Brands is big on diversity," said Winik. "We should take her to the races."

TWELVE

Dad asked Kyle to take Friday off from school and ride shotgun in the hauler with Billy, who had passed his heart tests and was feeling fine. Kyle didn't argue. Dad would work it out with the principal, an old friend. Some part of Kyle even liked the idea. Billy was a nice guy with good stories, but it was more than that. This could be payback for calling the sling, for getting Kris hurt. Then we're even and I can go blow my horn. Be the last practice I miss.

At breakfast Mom filled a plastic bag with sandwiches, fruit, cookies, and soda, as if he were going on a hunting trip instead of spending three hours in a truck.

"This is not going to happen again," she said. "This

73

is a special situation."

"Very special," said Dad. He looked haggard. He'd been up half the night with Kris and Uncle Kale, testing the car at Goshen Raceway. They'd fly to Monroe Speedway in a Family Brands plane. "This is a fresh beginning."

"That's a cereal," said Mom.

"Lynda." Dad held up his hands in the stop signal. "You set, Kyle?"

"Yeah." He had packed last night.

"Bring your helmet and shoes."

"Why?" snapped Mom.

"Just covering all bases," said Dad. "What if we need him to crew?"

"Kerry! This is a one-time deal." She enunciated each word as if she were talking to a child.

"One-time deal," said Dad.

Kyle felt a cold flicker in his gut. He tried to tune in to it. Was it fear? Excitement? He remembered the feeling from when he had raced. Sometimes he felt it before a brass performance. He let the flicker grow, fill his abdomen and chest. Felt good.

He'd felt it last night on the phone with Nicole, trying to explain how important this race was to the family. Talking about the new sponsors and the new paint job and the better engine, he'd felt that cold flicker, but she had smothered it with her indifference, her ignorance, what he considered her selfishness. She didn't know what he was talking about and didn't seem to care. She wanted to talk about the quintet, how he was letting them all down and what he was missing. He thought he and Nicole could have been talking from alternate universes.

And then she said, "I guess it's a guy thing, cars, right?"

He had thought of Jimmie and said, "There are women at the track."

"What do they call them, pit bunnies?"

He let it go, but soon after that the conversation was over.

After he clicked off, he wondered if he had failed to explain because he didn't fully understand himself. Maybe he was being swept along by the family. He was doing what they wanted, not what he wanted.

"Kyle?" Dad was staring at him.

"Just trying to remember where I put the helmet," he said.

"Been that long." Dad shook his head. "Seems like yesterday you won the state quarter-midget."

Six years ago, Kyle thought. Why bring that up? The cold flicker grew until it felt like a bird wing beating against his ribs.

"Always sorry you quit racing," said Dad. "Thought

you had a real—"

"Kerry!" This time Mom held up the stop sign.

"Family conference?" Kris stumbled into the kitchen. He was pale, bloodshot. Even his spiky black hair drooped.

"How'd you sleep?" asked Mom.

"Pill helped." He slumped into a chair. Kyle thought Mom and Dad made an effort not to look at each other.

The hauler's horn blared outside. Kyle said, "Better go. See you there." He nodded at Kris and Dad. Mom hugged him harder than usual.

He ran upstairs to get his helmet and shoes. He knew exactly where they were, in an old bowling bag near the front of his closet.

Billy McCall was smoking handmades and blasting the Grateful Dead. Is this the latest treatment for heart problems? Be a long trip, thought Kyle. He jammed in his iPod buds and cranked the volume until Dizzy drowned Jerry. They stopped at a store outside town to pick up the barbecue meat Billy would cook for the crew at the track, then hit the highway. They drove for more than an hour before Billy punched out the Dead CD and signaled Kyle to unplug his ears.

"Need my Dead fix to start every trip. What you listening to?"

"Dizzy Gillespie."

Billy grunted. "Miles the man. Could always calm Sir Walter down with *Sketches of Spain*."

Kyle caught Billy glancing at him from the corner of his eye and grinning. Am I showing the surprise I feel? "He listened to jazz?"

"Sometimes you got to get away from that she-stole-my-heart-and-my-pickup-too, 'specially if no fans around. Got to drive to your own music, right?" Billy had his eyes on the road again. "What's with Kris?"

"How do you mean?"

"He shaky or anything?"

"You notice something?"

"Just like your grandpa, cat and mouse."

"What do you know?"

"They were up all night repainting the right fender. Figured Kris scraped the wall."

"Happens."

"At Goshen? Wonder how come they weren't testing at Monroe. Makes more sense to try out a car on the speedway you'll be racing on than your little old hometown track." Billy seemed angry. "Unless something was wrong you didn't want people to know about. Usually it's something wrong with the car, not the driver."

Bring your helmet and shoes. That's what they tell the backup driver. But you need to be eighteen years old to drive in American Racing League–sanctioned events, so I can't fill in for Kris.

Billy wasn't finished. "How long I been working for Hildebrand Racing? Before you were born. Before your daddy started driving. They don't tell me nothing no more."

"Maybe they figured you too busy getting your tests and all."

That seemed to calm him down a little. "Yeah, maybe." Then he squinted at Kyle. "You don't think they're writing me off?"

"Seemed real glad you're going back upstairs today."

He chuckled at that. "After your little sling deal."

"Kale was pissed."

"Always gotta be in control, that boy. He's good, but prickly. Wouldn't've won without the sling."

"Or got hurt."

"Kale lay that on you?" Billy shook his head. "That was Slater's fault, plain and simple. That mean sonuvabitch needs to get a good neck stretching. Sir Walter loved the sling deal."

"He say that?" Kyle was surprised by the eagerness in his voice.

"Your grandpa told me you and Kris the best set of brothers since Ken and Kale." Billy coughed. "Meant to say Kerry and Kale."

Billy put the Grateful Dead back on.

THIRTEEN

Kyle got his first look at the new paint job after Billy pulled into their space in the Monroe Speedway garage area. He climbed in the back of the hauler and ran his hand over the smooth metal skin. The green-and-red Family Brands logos clashed with the Hildebrand deep blue, but maybe that was okay. He thought of a jazz riff, dissonant and forceful. The blue was the bass line, the red and green were trumpets. He couldn't decide if it was beautiful or ugly, but it got to him. The letters across the hood, Jump Start Your Life, seemed to shimmer.

"Kind of in your face," said Jimmie. He'd been so absorbed by the paint job, he hadn't heard her walk into the hauler. "What do you think?"

"Never judge a car by its paint job."

"Sounds wise. Kris here?" She sounded confident, like she thought she belonged.

"So what's your deal?" He heard the annoyance in his voice. Not cool. But it flared her nostrils. He liked being able to get to her.

"Same's everybody," she said. "I want to win."

"Who you think you are, just walk in and—"

"Hold on." A red flush rose on the pale skin of her neck. "Just 'cause you got the name don't mean you got the game."

"What's that supposed to mean?" He felt angry, but in control.

The flush had reached her clenched jaw. "You got the chance to be a Hildebrand driver and you'd rather be a band fag." Her eyes flicked over his shoulder, and her mouth snapped shut. Kyle turned to see Billy. He had heard the exchange.

"Give me a hand," said Billy. He avoided looking at them.

They rolled the car out of the hauler and through a crowd of crew members and fans milling along the main road of the garage area. Kyle didn't look at Jimmie as they pushed the car. What she had said didn't bother him; he had heard worse in the hallway at school, but he felt angry that she had felt confident enough to say it in a Hildebrand hauler. Who the hell was she?

Engines roared and whined, hammers banged on metal. Gas fumes and dots of debris stung Kyle's eyes and nostrils. They pushed the car across the road and into an enclosed bay reserved for Hildebrand Racing. Dad and Uncle Kale were waiting. They opened the hood and ducked their heads into the motor.

Kyle started back to the hauler to help Billy unload the rolling toolboxes, but Jimmie grabbed his arm. She had a strong grip. "I'm sorry. I had no right—"

He jerked his arm free. I'm not going to snap back at her and I'm not going to take her apology. She can go to hell.

"Hey, Kyle, introduce me." It was Ryder. He hip-checked Kyle out of his way and extended a hand to Jimmie. "You can call me Ruff."

"Call you meathead the way you drive," she said.

"Whoa, a redheaded ballbuster." Ryder laughed and backed off, hands up. "Enjoy the new paint, folks—I'll be scraping it off tomorrow."

"They'll be scraping you off the wall," said Jimmie.

Ryder looked like he didn't want to mess with Jimmie. He turned to glare at Kyle. "You got something to say?"

"Save it for the track," said Kyle. "You'll need it."

Ryder seemed to be measuring the distance between them. Would he swing? Kyle felt relaxed but alert reading him. He decided Ruff wouldn't do anything. The bully was confused.

"Kyle." Jackman loomed up, the crew behind him. Ryder cursed and stormed away. "What he want?"

"Just rubbin' around," said Jimmie. "Kyle set him straight."

"That's my boy." Jackman knuckled Kyle's head. It didn't feel good, but it was a small price for big old Jackoff having your back. "Let's look at the car."

Dad and Uncle Kale were still under the hood. Kris was in a corner fussing with his fire suit. He still looked lousy. When he spotted Kyle, he jerked his head and winked, but the old signal seemed more pleading than demanding. Something was wrong. Am I reading too much into this? Kyle strolled over.

Kris draped a limp arm over his shoulder. "Glad you're here, li'l bro."

He climbed up to the top of the grandstand for Kris's test laps, as much to get away from everybody as for the view. The car performed well enough, smooth and steady on the straightaways, no sign of looseness or push in the turns, but Kris never opened it up. Kyle figured they must be massaging the new engine. Time enough to let it rip in the qualifying run, when speed mattered.

Kyle saw a flash of red hair down in the pits. How had she moved in? Gives me crap, then props in front of Jackman. What was her game? Hildebrand Racing had always been a closed shop. Even Jackman and Billy were related to the family, by marriage but still related. And she just prances around like she belongs. Who is she related to? Or sleeping with?

Kris was the thirty-first of forty-six signed up to qualify for thirty spots. The track would be a mess, grooved and littered with rubber and bits of metal, but he'd have the advantage of knowing what most everybody else had done, whose time he'd need to beat for better position. Ruff and Gary had run fast times. Slater had run fast enough to qualify in a decent position.

Kris's run was cautious. You'd never have known The Intruder was at the wheel. He stayed away from the wall and braked easily on the turns. Be lucky to place in the top twenty. Was there a strategy here? Were they playing possum so nobody would know what they had under the hood, trying to lull the opposition into overconfidence, then blast by them in the final laps?

No one told me, he thought. I'm outside the loop with Billy. But isn't that what I want? Dad had invited him over to Goshen Raceway last night to watch Kris test the car, but he'd said he was too busy. Quintet practice.

You want to know what's going on, band fag, go ask the redheaded ballbuster.

FOURTEEN

He stayed up in the grandstand for a while, enjoying being alone as the sweet, warm afternoon cooled into a soft evening. By the time he got down to the garage area, number 12 was back in its bay and Uncle Kale was back under its hood. Jackman was handing him tools. Across the road Jimmie and the crew were standing by the hauler, drinking Jump and eating Chaco Chips while Billy fired up his barbecue grill and his Crock-Pot for supper.

Billy spotted him. "Kerry wants you back at the motel." There was something anxious in his face.

"What's up?"

"You see how Kris qualified?"

"That wasn't the plan?"

Billy shook his head. "You better talk to your dad."

The motel was on the highway south of the speed-way, a quarter mile away, but Kyle shouldered his bag and walked. Need to stretch out my legs, he thought. Or delay what was coming up. Did they know yesterday after Kris drove the car at Goshen? The talk at break-fast. Bring your helmet and shoes. Sorry you quit racing.

But you need to be eighteen to drive in an ARL-sanctioned race at this level. So I'm safe, right?

Am I sure I want to be safe?

They had connecting rooms at the motel. He went into the one with the open door. Dad was sitting in a chair, staring at the wall. He held a finger to his lips and pointed to the doorway that led to the next room. Kris was on a bed, snoring. Dad signaled Kyle to close the door.

"Boyd's available if we need him," said Dad.

"For what?" said Kyle, stalling.

"Kris had trouble controlling the car last night, scraped the wall. Lost concentration. I thought his head might clear. Kidding myself." He looked at Kyle. "Too risky for him to race. We could get Boyd. Family Brands rather have you or me."

"Don't you have to be eighteen?"

"They can get a waiver. Be just for one race."

"Been so long." He wasn't sure what he wanted to say. Been much longer for Dad.

"Since you weren't the one who qualified, you'd have to start dead last. No pressure. Stay out of trouble, move up slow, you got three hundred laps. You finish in the top twenty-five, everybody be happy."

Like I have a choice. "One race."

Dad smiled. "Let's order some room service. Make a plan."

The burgers and fries came up quickly. Dad seemed to be searching for a way to begin. "Means a lot to me, you doing this." Then he got quiet for a moment. "I know what you're going through." Quiet again. Kyle thought of a car starting and stalling. "There were other things I wanted to do, too." Stall.

"What kind of things?"

Dad shrugged. "Build stuff. Bridges. In foreign countries. I'd just started college, thinking about engineering school, when Ken joined the army. Your grandpa was winding down by then. He wanted to retire, but he wouldn't until there was another Hildebrand in his number twelve."

"You had no choice?"

It was a question, but Dad said, "You understand."

"Not really."

Dad sighed. "Ken was good, really good. He and Kale

were a great team. But Ken and Sir Walter butted heads and Ken took off. Sir Walter won't even mention his name. Two stubborn men. Sad."

Kyle had heard pieces of the story before. Grandma Karen had stayed in contact with Ken over the years, even saw him and his family secretly a few times. Ken had been in Afghanistan with the Rangers when Grandma died, and never made it to the funeral. Mom and Dad still exchanged cards and e-mails with Ken and his wife and kids. Last they heard, Ken was a master sergeant, in Iraq.

"So you replaced Ken." Just saying that made Kyle shiver.

Dad nodded. Kyle could tell he didn't want to talk about it anymore. Dad said, "We better talk about that third turn, the one with the little dogleg. Want to tuck you in early. Big day."

He was exhausted, but he couldn't sleep. He would drift to the edge of the precipice, but the moment he willed himself to roll over into sleep, he would be wide-awake. He had stuffed orange plugs into his ears to muffle Kris's wheezing and moaning in the next bed, but they seemed to amplify the thoughts rattling around his head.

He was scared.

Not about driving. He could handle the car and the track, and as long as he wasn't expected to go door to door with Gary and Ruff and Slater and finish in the top ten, he'd be okay.

He was scared of being sucked in, trapped, dragged along. You had no choice? You understand.

Just one race?

What if Kris wasn't ready next week? And the week after that?

So why didn't you say, No. Boyd's available.

How could you let that red ass take a Hildebrand seat?

That's not your problem.

Dad could drive number 12 this weekend. He did it for years after the accident, when he didn't have his chops anymore. Kyle was about seven when it happened, Kris nine, both already racing. They loved to watch Dad drive. They had seen the wreck. It was a Big One, spectacular, Red Hoyt's car slamming into the wall, then tumbling across the track, wiping out half a dozen cars. Dad had been hit, but he'd kept control. He seemed to be driving out of danger when Mom screamed and pointed at the flames licking up from his front wheels. The fire suits weren't as good in those days, or maybe the heat was just too intense. By the time they pulled him out of the car, he'd been burned from his ankles to his hips.

It would have been a scarier time if the family hadn't pulled together. Aunt Susan took care of Kyle and Kris so Mom could be at the hospital all the time. When Dad was discharged, Billy McCall drove him to physical therapy every day and waited and drove him home. Sir Walter got back into number 12 so the money would keep coming in. Jackman's mom and dad were among a dozen relatives who made sure there was always dinner on the table.

Uncle Ken showed up, sneaked in and out one night. Dad was on heavy painkillers, and for a long time he thought it had been a dream, his older brother in uniform standing by his hospital bed squeezing his hand.

That was the only time Kyle ever saw Uncle Ken. He stopped by the house to look at his nephews. He was almost as tall as Dad, broad like Uncle Kale but not fat, a voice as deep as Sir Walter's. His chest was filled with ribbons. He hugged Kyle and Kris. They both remembered his medals digging through their pajamas. Kyle thought Uncle Ken was crying, but Kris said that was impossible. Hildebrand men never cry. And then Uncle Ken was gone.

Everybody was amazed at how quick a recovery Dad made. He was back in number 12 the following season. But he shouldn't have been driving. He was still in pain from the burn scars and not as confident as he needed to be in tight spots. He drove for three more seasons, never winning, rarely even getting into the top ten.

He shouldn't be replacing Kris now.

Maybe this is what you really want, Kyle. Look how you got off at being the family hero last week steering Kris over the line. You loved the attention.

Maybe all this trumpet noise is just a cover. What you really want is Kris's gig as golden boy.

Do you want to be compared to him? Rookie of the year last season, hot young driver this season, Sexiest Newcomer on the NASCAR Scene website.

And in this corner, li'l bro, Kylie the Band Fag.

He called Nicole.

As soon as she answered, he knew it was a mistake, but it was too late to hang up.

"Where are you?" She sounded sleepy.

"Monroe. Sorry, I forgot what time . . . ."

"No problem. We had an awesome practice tonight. We really sounded tight." Her voice shifted gears. "I mean, as much as a quintet can with only four instruments." It sounded tacked on, as if she didn't really mean it. Were they a quartet now? "We just fell into this amazing thing, jazz riffs off the 'Pavane.' Todd started it, and we were all wailing."

He tried to seem enthusiastic. "Sounds great."

"When will you be back?"

"I'm driving tomorrow."

"Driving back? Great."

"In the race. I'm driving number twelve in the NoCaBank 300."

"You're racing? What about Kris?"

"He's not recovered." When she didn't say anything, he added, "From the crash."

"You told me you quit racing." He thought she sounded angry.

"I did. I'm his backup."

"For how long?"

"Just this race."

"What if he can't drive next week?"

"I don't know."

"What about the quintet?"

"Sounds like you're doing fine without me." He heard the anger in his own voice.

"Would have been better with you, Kyle. What's going on? I thought you were serious about music."

"I am."

"You're giving it up to race."

"Just because I race cars doesn't mean"—he searched for what he meant—"I'm not still a band fag."

She laughed. "At least you haven't lost your sense of humor," she said.

"I better get some sleep," he said. "Sorry I woke you up."

"Good luck tomorrow." She sounded like she meant it.

"Thanks." He wanted to say more, but she hung up.

He suddenly felt very lonely. He listened to Kris snoring. The wheezing and moaning had stopped. He wished Kris would wake up. They could talk about tomorrow's race. He knew the track.

Maybe I'll surprise them tomorrow.

Yeah, right. Maybe I'll wreck. Maybe I'll start the Big One.

Got to try to sleep.

He forced his mind away from racing, away from Nicole, and it settled into "Pavane for a Dead Princess," and he was hitting and holding that beautiful line, his fingers on the cool mother-of-pearl buttons, his lips vibrating with the good pain that made pure sound.

The sound filled his head until the drums came in.

There were no drums in this piece.

Dad was knocking on the door.

The big day had begun.

He had never gotten this kind of attention before, not at ten when he won the county quarter-midget title for twelve-and-unders, not at eleven when he won the state for under-fourteen, not at fifteen when he was running in the top ten in modifieds and sprint cars against drivers Dad's age, just before he tried late models and then quit. The attention embarrassed him, but he liked it.

At breakfast Uncle Kale, Jackman, and Dad moved around the table so Winik and Sir Walter could sit on either side of him. He was glad Kris was still upstairs, sleeping. He might feel bad. Replaced.

When the waitress spotted Sir Walter, she rushed over with a pot of coffee. "Fresh brewed, Sir Walter." She giggled like a kid. She could have been Sir Walter's age.

"Well, thank you"—Sir Walter squinted at the name tag on her chest—"Sheri. But today the race driver gets served first. Say hello to my grandson Kyle."

"Hi, Kyle." She poured his coffee. "Got enough cream, sugar?"

When everybody laughed, Kyle realized she was calling him Sugar. "Take it black."

"Just like Sir Walter," she said. "Hope you drive like him."

"Give him time, Sheri—he's gonna be better." Sir Walter waited until she had poured everyone's coffee before he reached into the shirt pocket where he kept his Sharpie pens.

"I wasn't gonna bother you," said Sheri.

"Never a bother." Sir Walter slowly signed a menu for her in his elegant handwriting. *For Sheri, Jump start your life, Sir Walter Hildebrand, No. 12.*

What happened to *Keep your eyes on the road ahead*?

Family Brands happened.

Sheri pressed the menu to her chest, blew Sir Walter a kiss, and ran off.

Winik nudged Kyle. "Work on your penmanship."

"Sure Kris can't make it?" Uncle Kale sounded pissed off.

"Let's go check tires," said Dad, standing up, signaling

Kale to come with him.

"Ain't had my breakfast," said Uncle Kale.

Wouldn't hurt you to miss a few meals, thought Kyle. Uncle Kale glared at him as if he had read his mind, then glared at Dad, who was gathering up his laptop and binders. Uncle Kale was the older brother, but Dad was the president of Hildebrand Racing, in charge of everything that didn't have to do with the car and the race itself, which was the crew chief's domain. They usually worked out their differences privately, but this was starting to look like a public tug-of-war.

Sir Walter cleared his throat. "Billy will make you something at the garage, Kale."

Uncle Kale stood up and said, "See you all over there."

Sir Walter waited until they had left the dining room before he turned to Winik and said, "Crew chiefs get used to a driver. Hard to make a change."

"Just for one race, right?" said Winik.

"Right," said Sir Walter, but it didn't sound convincing to Kyle. What did he know? "Now, let's order, Kyle. We need to stop by the Family Brands tent, visit with the folks, take some pictures."

Kyle wasn't hungry. He picked at his omelet, pushed home fries around the plate. People stopped to talk to Sir Walter, ask for an autograph, and he made sure to introduce every one of them to Kyle. One woman pinched Kyle's cheek, and Sir Walter laughed out loud.

On the way out, Sir Walter whispered, "You should eat, but you have to drink water. Gonna lose a lot in the car."

A Family Brands van was waiting for them outside the motel. It took a back road to the speedway to avoid the traffic, and went in through a gate marked NO ENTRANCE. A state trooper dragged away a wooden saw-horse barrier to let them through. They drove beyond the parking lots to an exhibition area, dozens of trailers selling caps and die-cast cars, a village of big white tents where the sponsors, UPS and Miller Lite and the Air Force and Kellogg's, entertained their guests. Bands played and balloons bumped against each other in the gentle morning breeze. Winik led them into the Family Brands tent, big as a school gym. People piled their plates at a buffet breakfast spread before taking them to long tables. A bluegrass band strummed on a small stage.

Sir Walter put his mouth to Kyle's ear and said, "All you got to say, 'Thanks, I'll do my best for my family and Family Brands.' Got it?" Before Kyle could nod, Sir Walter clapped his shoulder and pushed himself up on the stage.

The band gave Sir Walter a fanfare. He waved while

Winik put on a number 12 cap, grabbed the mic, and shouted, "A great honor to give you a great driver, a great American, and a great representative for a great company, Sir Walter Hildebrand."

Sir Walter took the mic, smiled, and nodded at the stomping and hollering crowd. "Pleasure to visit with you folks—makes me feel like part of your family, too. Know you got some serious eating to do this morning, so I won't take but a minute more of your time to introduce the face of the future, a fourth-generation racin' man, my grandson Kyle Hildebrand."

Kyle nearly tripped getting up onstage. He stumbled toward Sir Walter, who handed him the mic, which almost slipped out of his sweaty hand. Could it get worse?

But once he had the mic in his hand, staring out at all those smiling faces, he settled down. Just like taking a trumpet solo in the auditorium.

"Thanks. I'll do my best for you out there today, for Hildebrand and for Family Brands." And then, before he thought about it, he shouted, "Jump start your life!"

The crowd yelled and clapped. Grandpa squeezed his shoulder, and Winik looked up at him across the stage and raised a thumb.

Felt good.

SIXTEEN

He sensed the freeze right away as he walked into the big room off the official inspection garage for the drivers' meeting. He was surrounded by Dad, Uncle Kale, and Jackman, but they couldn't shut out the low grumbles and the hard stares. Nobody likes rookies—Kyle knew that. They are unpredictable, they make mistakes, they get in the way, they cause wrecks. The track tapes a yellow stripe across a rookie's back bumper as a warning. Stay away from this one; he doesn't know what he's doing.

Last year Kris had worn his yellow stripe like a screw-you bumper sticker, daring other drivers to mess with him. He won more races than anyone else that season, the first time a rookie ever did that. Do they want to take it out on me? They should be glad it's me they have to race against instead of him, Kyle thought. Hey, that's not constructive thinking.

Jackman shouldered open a path toward the front of the garage. Drivers and crew chiefs muttered, but they got out of the way. Boyd Jurgensen, who was almost as big as Jackman, bumped shoulders and glared at Kyle. His uniform was as white as his car, still no big sponsor. Kyle wondered if he was angry that he hadn't gotten Kris's seat. Would they really have given it to him, or was that just a way of putting more pressure on me?

A few of the older drivers and crew chiefs gave Dad friendly nods.

"Luck, Kyle." It was old Randall Bean, hand out. Gratefully, Kyle shook it.

"Maybe you two can draft up," said Ruff, "and stay out of our way."

Randall's fists came up, but a track official stepped in and said, "Any behavior, boys, and you'll be watching the race from your trailer."

Ruff grinned and turned away. The track official pushed his way to a small clearing in the front of the room and climbed up on a metal folding chair. He had to shout to be heard over the jittery chatter.

"Got a visitor, men, from headquarters. Ben Dutton."

That quieted them down. Dutton, tall and wide, didn't

need to stand on a chair. His voice boomed off the metal and stone walls.

"We don't like what we saw last week. That chicken-shit deal at the finish got no place in big-league racin'. Simple rules. You get beat fair, you take it like a man. Nobody wrecks out of spite. Anybody carries this into this week, I'm here to tell you there'll be penalties, now and up the road, not to mention we'll be up your tailpipe. Hard racin' but clean racin'. Any questions?"

"I got one." It was Gary Nagle. "Been bad wrecks here, you never come down. This about Family Brands and the waiver for Baby Hildebrand?"

There was applause from the crowd and a few whistles.

Jackman and Uncle Kale exchanged glances. Dad put a hand on Kyle's shoulder. "It's about last week, Kyle, not about you."

Dutton's big face got red and hard. "Glad you asked that question, clear the air. What's your name, son?"

There were a few laughs as Gary hesitated. He looked sorry he had opened his mouth. "Gary Nagle."

"I know you, Gary, promising young driver, got the stones to speak your mind. Look forward to seeing you in the Cup series someday." Dutton was smooth and tough. "Now I got a question for you, Gary. You want to grow this sport? You want more high-class sponsors to come in, more big-league advertisers? What happened last week gave us the kind of black eye those knuckle-head ballplayers give their so-called sports."

There were a few laughs at that. Kyle sensed the angry mood starting to lift. Without answering Gary's question directly, Dutton had taken control. Kyle was impressed. This was a taste of the big leagues.

"Let's see some racin' today," said Dutton. "Bangin' and rubbin's part of the deal, but not spinnin' somebody into the wall 'cause you can. Good luck."

The local track official climbed back up on the chair and reminded them that a race can't be won on the first lap and that anyone who came into the pit road at more than thirty-five miles an hour would be black-flagged to the end of the longest line.

The track chaplain offered a short prayer that no one would be hurt, and then they were back out into the overcast day, dicey racing weather. Never know when the sun might come out and change the conditions of the track.

"You see Slater?" said Dad.

"Hiding in the back," said Uncle Kale. "Ain't heard the last of that dingleberry."

"Remind Billy to keep an eye on him," said Dad.

Jackman said, "Maybe I should just remind Slater that—"

"You got enough to do," said Uncle Kale, "reminding your boys to hold on to their gas cans."

They were almost at the hauler, already smelling Billy's barbecue, when a woman jumped out of the crowd, dodged around Jackman, and thrust her chest into Kyle's face. Puppy-size boobs bumped around inside a number 12 T-shirt. "Sign my shirt, Kris?"

While Kyle hesitated, unsure what to do, Uncle Kale snickered and said, "Sorry, lady, this here's Kyle."

"That's okay," she said, waving her Sharpie.

Kyle was wondering what Sir Walter would have done when Jackman pulled him away, leaving the woman behind.

"Lesson for you," said Uncle Kale. "Drivers are interchangeable. Like a monkey in a rocket ship. It's the car, stupid."

SEVENTEEN

In the moment before the green flag dropped, he felt icy prickles cascade down his back and skitter out along his arms and legs. Like before a concert. Once he blew his first note, the prickles would melt and he'd be in the zone, that deep cave of calm. His mouth was dry. That didn't matter here. The white noise of the roaring crowd and the growling engines was shredded by radio static.

"Stay awake, Kylie," said Uncle Kale.

"Up yours," he said before he thought about it. But it didn't matter. He had forgotten to press the talk-back button on the wheel, so nobody heard him. Wonder what else I'm forgetting to do. Stay awake, Kylie.

"Nice and easy, Kyle," said Dad. "Nobody wins in the first lap."

Even with a rolling start, it took Kyle a lap to get to speed. There were twenty-nine cars ahead of him.

Nice and easy. Nobody wins a 150-mile race in the first lap. And I'm not here to win, not even to make the top ten, just here to keep Kris's seat warm, get some team points toward the championship by finishing all three hundred laps. The race was going to be on regional TV. ESPN might put some of it into a national feed. Family Brands would like that.

"Stay alert now, Kylie."

The early laps were slow but steady. From the tachometer he figured he was doing about seventy-five miles per hour, stuck behind the Clot. That's what Uncle Kale called the strokers near the end of the field, blockages in the bloodstream of a race, losers in a bunch. There were really four races going on. Up front were the leaders, maybe half a dozen racers with a real chance to win; then the Pack, a dozen also-rans who might get up there; then the Clot; and finally the Stragglers in sick cars just trying to finish.

Kris would have dissolved the Clot by now, ripped right through them. Get stuck behind the Clot, Kris would say, you might as well hang your head out the window and work on your tan.

There were about a dozen in the Clot.

Kyle drove right into the middle of it.

"Easy, Kyle, you're three wide," said Billy from the grandstand roof.

For a lap he was boxed in, never a good idea with these clowns. He kept looking for daylight, waiting for someone to blink. A black-and-yellow Chevy bobbled and moved up a lane, and he shot through the space. He picked off another one. Number 12 wanted to run. Horses under this hood. He passed a third car.

"Nice," said Billy. "You got Casper the Ghost coming up on your right." His voice sounded a little thick. Was it him or the radio?

Kyle mashed the gas and left Boyd's white car behind. Suddenly he was leading the Clot. Up ahead, the Pack loomed.

"Clear both sides," said Billy.

Uncle Kale said, "Take your time."

He took his time. He spent fifty laps between the Pack and the Clot, concentrating on establishing his territory and holding it, finding that comfortable groove on the surface of the track that suited his car. He was learning the track as he dove into the turns, braking to let the car rotate so he could drop down into the straightaways. Between the Pack and the Clot, with no one trying to pass, he could focus on driving. After a while the Pack began breaking into single file. Randall was falling back. He came alongside, smoking slightly.

As Kyle passed him, the old man gave a little wave. At least one friend out here.

He pressed the button. "Where am I?"

"Nineteen," said Billy.

"That's good," said Dad. "Stay there."

"How's she feel?" said Uncle Kale.

"Twitchy."

"Let's see what you got," said Uncle Kale.

Kyle took a deep breath and eased up behind a purple Toyota with a yellow rookie stripe hanging at the bottom of the track. He didn't want Kyle to pass him. Feint left, feint right, but purple Toyota stayed with him, blocking the pass. That was Lloyd Rogers, a good open-wheel driver who had come over from Indy cars. He was a black guy whom ARL was showing off as part of its diversity program. Lloyd wasn't going to let another rookie get around him, even if he was driving number 12. Especially if he was driving number 12.

Out of my way, rookie, thought Kyle. You think I'm going to back off for you. Kyle swerved left and right, but purple Toyota stayed with him. He could drive.

"Easy, Kyle," said Dad. "You're fine where you are."

No, I'm not. He felt juiced and jittery, sweating under the fire suit but chilly, too. Felt good.

Kyle let purple Toyota settle back into his groove, then tapped the accelerator. He bumped purple Toyota lightly, flush on the back bumper, not so much a hit as a hello. Then he dropped back.

"Kyle!" said Dad.

Purple Toyota held his line. Okay, you asked for it. This time, Kyle bumped him hard. Purple Toyota swerved toward the wall, and while he was getting his car back under control, Kyle whipped past on the inside. He felt a rush of pure pleasure.

"Twitchy all right," said Uncle Kale. "Come on in now, tires and gas. Speed limit's thirty-five, don't blow it."

He was feeling too good to let Uncle Kale bother him.

EIGHTEEN

He downshifted to second gear and braked hard into the pit road, cars streaming in behind him. As he slid into the pit stall, Jackman leaped over the wall, the crew charging after him like Super Troopers, yelling at each other and grinning. Kyle knew the feeling. They felt like they were in the race. He pulled on the mesh screen to let the water pole in and grabbed the cup. Some of the water made it into his mouth, some onto his chest. He saw a flash of red hair on the other side of the water pole. What was she doing here?

He felt the car jerk and drop as the tires were changed, heard the thud of the gas can flung back over the wall. The crew were yelling instructions at each other. They were hitting their marks perfectly today. He thought about the quintet playing tight.

"Kyle?" It was Dad. "How you feel?"

"She wants to run."

"How *you* feel?"

"I'm fine."

"You're doing good," said Dad. "Don't push it."

"You think she can pick off a few more," said Uncle Kale, "go for it. Okay, thirty-five hundred until you're out."

Ruff pulled in front of him on the pit road and flipped a finger. Kyle slowed to avoid bumping him, and the green Ford, Slater, came right up behind him, almost touching. For a moment he was trapped between them. It was a message. Watch yourself, Baby Hildebrand. Then Ruff accelerated onto the track and Kyle followed him.

It took him a while to work his way back up to nineteen, but this time the Pack was running three wide again and it was harder to advance. He wondered why Billy wasn't talking. Could use some spotting about now.

"Where's Gary and Ruff?"

"Don't worry about them," said Dad.

"They been trading the lead," said Uncle Kale. "Slater's up there too."

Don't even think about. You're in nineteenth place.

With a little patience and luck you might even get a shot at the top fifteen. That would be great.

Be something to make top ten. Maybe even . . .

You're just here to keep Kris's seat warm, then get your seat back in the quintet. Right?

For the next few laps he concentrated on finding his line and holding it. He kept alert for a chance to move up. He passed a car with an overheated engine. He blocked Boyd coming up behind him in the white car.

He sensed something wrong up ahead. The Pack felt loose and wobbly. Wish Billy would give a shout. He thought he saw a thin plume of smoke. Maybe it was just dark dust kicked up by wind. Cars weren't holding their lines. Too much bobbing and weaving. He gripped the wheel hard, ready to twist it.

He began to imagine the wreck.

In his mind the wreck was unfolding at the top of the Pack, a car pushed too hard was about to spin or bobble, and the cars behind checked up. The Big One. Everybody behind would get a piece, no one would escape, the only question was how bad. Where's Billy? I need those eyes on the roof.

"Go to the wall," said a voice he didn't recognize.

"What?"

"Billy had to leave." He recognized the voice even before she said, "It's Jimmie. Go high—there's room."

He could trust her or not. No time for debate. He turned right, taking the car right up to the wall before he swerved along it, scraping the wall, watching sparks splash off his door and fly past his window. He had just enough room between the wall and a black Dodge to slip through.

Now the wreck he had imagined was unfolding right in front of him. Cars were spinning off to the grass, climbing over each other, metal screaming as it tore. Better slow down before I plow right into the middle of it.

Her voice was very calm. "Mash it, Kyle. Boyd's on your back and you got a hole."

He stamped on the accelerator and drove into a pea-soup fog, billowing white smoke that rose and fell like a flapping curtain. He saw flashes of paint, red, yellow, blue, never a whole car. He braced himself for a crash.

"Go low, hard, now."

He wrenched the wheel left. A yellow wall loomed up, filled his windshield, dropped away, clipping his right front fender just enough to spin him right.

"Right, right, stay with it."

He wrenched the wheel right and floated through the path cleared by the yellow car.

"Clear low off the wall."

He twisted left, giving himself up to the voice in his

ears, letting it push him like a needle through cloth, letting it play him like an instrument, trusting his life to it. Smoke and fumes filled his nose and mouth. His head pounded.

"Straighten out along the grass."

And then they were through the wreck, the leaders up ahead, half a dozen cars untouched by the wreck. There was a smoking junkyard in his rearview mirror. Rescue crews rushed out onto the track.

The field froze in place as the red flag dropped.

"Man, you drove the hell out of it," said Jimmie.

He wished he could see her face. Maybe even touch it. He wanted to tell her she had been in the car with him. Four hands on the wheel. The best he could do was "Great spotting." It sounded weak.

"Thanks," she said. She sounded grateful.

NINETEEN

By the time they were racing again under a green flag, shadows stretched across the track and the air had cooled. Fifteen cars had been towed off and only six of those had come back to race. Nobody had been seriously hurt. When that was announced, the crowd stood up and cheered for five minutes. Fans love their wrecks, Kyle thought, but they can't stand the sight of blood.

With thirty laps to go, he was in ninth place. Sounded better than it was, he thought, with only twenty-one cars left running.

"I can move up."

"You hold your place," snapped Dad.

He almost expected Jimmie to pipe up then, to tell Dad that Kyle had earned the right to go for it. That they owed it to the car. Why would I think she'd do that? She'd been pretty quiet since the wreck.

Two of the cars that had made it back from the wreck sprang leaks. Nineteen left racing. Kyle moved up to eighth, then seventh. He was surprised to see the green Ford in front of him. Slater was in sixth place, about two car lengths ahead. Be something to pass him and tell him, This is for Kris.

Dad must have read his mind. "Stay there, Kyle."

He wished he could talk to Jimmie on a private frequency. She could help him pass Slater. That had been awesome, her voice guiding him. Like to hear it again.

Focus.

It took two laps to get up behind Slater, who began weaving to block him. Kyle feinted to the outside, but Slater read the bluff and didn't react. Slater wasn't going to be easy to pass.

"Kyle."

You don't like the way I drive, Dad, come take the wheel.

"Boyd's coming up low," said Jimmie.

Should have seen that—I'm not staying alert. Hot. Tired.

He concentrated on blocking the white car moving up on his left. If Boyd passed him and then couldn't pass Slater, Kyle would be stuck in eighth with two cars right in front of him.

Twenty laps of racing left. Settle for seventh place? Family Brands be happy with that, Sir Walter and Dad too. I did my job, kept Kris's seat warm, scored some points for the team. Let me go back to the quintet now.

Get past Slater, you'll have a shot at the top five. That would be something.

"Green Ford's loose," said Jimmie.

The green Ford's rear end was waggling up toward the wall, and Slater seemed to be struggling to control it. Same thing happened at the end of last week's race when Kris was running alongside Slater, then slung past Ruff and Gary to win.

Kyle felt chills. Wouldn't that be a bitch. C'mon, now. Even if you get past Slater, no way you're gonna get past five more cars.

"You're clear both sides," said Jimmie. Reading my mind.

He waited another lap for the dogleg turn. There was more room to maneuver there. Slater's rear end floated up toward the wall and he turned right to straighten the green Ford.

Kyle shot past him on the inside.

On the next turn he could see the five cars ahead of him.

Ruff Ryder's brick-red number 22 Dodge and Gary

Nagle's number 24 light-blue Chevy were racing two wide for the lead. The next three cars were in single file. Just might pick off number 5, that purple Toyota he'd tapped out of his way early in the race. How did he get up there?

Well, I'm just going to have to move you again, rookie.

It took him four laps to catch up to the purple Toyota. Rogers started his blocking weave again. He wasn't giving up an inch.

"Don't push it, Kyle," said Dad. "You're good where you are."

He followed the purple Toyota for another four laps, waiting for his moment. Like the Blue Shadow, he thought.

"Boyd coming up low, Slater high," said Jimmie.

Kyle felt them almost before he saw them, the air changing around the car. He gripped the wheel harder as number 12 rocked. He couldn't let them box him in with the purple Toyota ahead. He swerved left. Boyd dropped back to avoid a crash. Enough room to try to pass the purple Toyota on the inside, but he quickly dropped down to block Kyle.

Kyle began to turn right.

"No, Slater's outside," yelled Jimmie.

Too late. He had made his move.

Incredibly, Slater let Kyle slide ahead of him.

Then he slammed Kyle into the wall.

It seemed to happen in slow motion. He saw the sudden opening between purple and green, turned right to drive into it, felt triumph bubble up as number 12 lunged through the hole. Slater was dropping back and Kyle was alongside the purple Toyota now, almost door to door, just about to pass him and take over fifth place, when Slater hit him.

It was a glancing bump on his left rear fender, perfectly executed to spin him right into the wall. His right front fender crashed into the wall. The car bounced back, stalled, died.

He tried to restart the car. It sputtered and died.

He could see the finish line up ahead. Ruff, then Gary crossed under a checkered flag. Boyd and Slater were past him. What was left of the Pack and the Clot were coming up. He would be even worse than last, he would never finish, just sit here a few yards from the end of the line.

Cars filled his rearview mirror, streamed around him, then filled his windshield.

He got hit. Bounced forward. Hit again.

"Go neutral," said Jimmie. "Turn the wheel left."

Numbly he followed her orders, shifting to neutral and twisting the wheel.

The third hit straightened him out. Yellow filled his rearview.

"Start it."

He flipped the toggle switch just as the yellow car hit him for the fourth time. The engine turned over, caught, he was moving. Old Randall Bean waved as the two of them crossed the finish line together under the checkered flag.

TWENTY

Billy was collapsed in one of the two reclining chairs in the back of the Family Brands jet, his thick arms hanging limply off the sides, his number 12 cap covering his face. The cap inflated and collapsed with his heavy breathing.

Kris was in the other chair, pale and quiet, staring at a DVD of the race on a TV screen.

They looked like they were in the wreck, thought Kyle. He was sitting in the main cabin with Dad, who was talking to Mom on the phone. Besides the pilots, there were just the four of them and the flight attendant on the plane. Sir Walter and the suits had stayed in Monroe for a meeting. The plane would go back for them later. Jackman would drive the hauler home.

Dad put the phone down. He sighed and rolled his eyes. Must have gotten an earful. Mom could let things go for a while, especially where the Hildebrand family was involved, but once she put her foot down, she could be as tough as any of them. Without her, he never would have been able to quit racing.

She had known what "bring your shoes and helmet" meant and let it go because Dad promised it was a special situation. A one-time deal. Well, now the one-time was over. No more deals.

Kyle imagined her end of the phone conversation. No more racing for Kyle. Get another driver if Kris isn't ready. Get Boyd.

Back to the quintet, thought Kyle. Focus on the trumpet. And Nicole.

He was free. He wondered why he didn't feel lighter.

Dad picked up the phone again. He was calling Billy's wife to tell her what time they'd be home. A doctor at the track had given Billy intravenous fluids and a sedative. He had pushed himself too far too fast. He'd be fine, just needed some rest.

Kyle had seen Jimmie only for an instant after the race, back in the garage area. She was helping the crew roll the car back into the hauler. The best he could do was raise his fist and mouth, "Thanks."

She smiled back, and the way that seemed to light up

her face, even light up her red hair, made Kyle's stomach turn over. Then she was gone, and Dad was pulling him into the van.

He wanted to hear her voice.

When the flight attendant came by with a loaded tray, Kyle picked out a sandwich and asked for a beer, trying to sound casual, not even choosing a brand. Would she ask his age? She was right back with three different brands and a big smile. "Watching you come through that wreck, I tell you my heart was in my mouth."

"You saw it?"

"We were in the Family Brands suite." She was pretty, not that much older than Kyle. He had the feeling that if he asked her what she was doing tonight, she might say she was free. She doesn't think she's talking to a high-school boy, he thought, she's talking to a driver. "Were you scared?"

"Too busy then," he said. "Afterward scared spitless."

She laughed, as if it were the smartest thing she had ever heard, and touched his arm. Dad was off the phone. When he saw Kyle sucking on a beer, he said, "I'll have one too."

Dad took a pull on his beer, then opened his laptop.

Kyle wanted to talk to Dad about the race. There hadn't been time afterward. They'd been too busy getting

Billy and Kris into the van and then onto the plane. Dad wanted to get them back home as quickly as possible. And now he was deep into the figures on his screen. Kyle tried to think of something to say. He wanted to talk about the final laps. What could he have done differently?

Dad looked up. "Forget about it."

How can he read my mind? "What?"

"Keep your eyes on the road ahead."

"Sir Walter doesn't say that anymore."

"Still beats mirror driving, always looking at what's behind you in the rearview mirror, where you came from instead of where you're going." He closed the laptop. "Stop kicking yourself. Nothing else you could do."

"Shouldn't've tried to pass Slater."

"Maybe shouldn't've tried to pass him the way you did. That's experience. I think you did good."

"You do?" That surprised him.

"Everybody does. Your grandpa liked the way you were picking off cars, one by one, Blue Shadow style. You know what your uncle Kale said? 'The kid was out there to win, and you can't teach that.'"

"Uncle Kale said that?"

Dad nodded. Kyle wanted to keep talking. Before Dad could open the laptop, Kyle said, "Kris be able to race?"

"Sure hope so. Got some more tests."

"What if he can't?"

Dad sighed. Kyle could tell he didn't want to talk about that. His fingers began tugging on the laptop lid. "Like Great-grandpa Fred used to say, we'll cross that bridge when we get over it."

"How come Jimmie took over?" He liked saying her name out loud.

"When Billy got quiet, we sent her up to see what was going on. She got the VIP guard to bring Billy back down, and she stayed to spot. Girl has a mind of her own." He grinned. "Like her grandpa."

"Who was that?"

"Red Hoyt." Dad's eyes widened. "You didn't know that?"

"So it wasn't Kris got her in."

"You kidding? Red was your grandpa's best friend. He called Jimmie his godgrandchild. She's got oil in her veins." He chuckled. "Some of Red's attitude, too, I hear."

"So she just showed up one day?"

"Sir Walter must've heard somewhere she dropped out of school and was working on cars, so he asked me to call her. Figured we'd be expanding the operation. You got a problem?"

"No, she got me through the wreck."

"Great job. And the way you responded, Kyle, that's something else you can't teach." He opened the laptop and peered at the screen. "I could've figured the gas smarter. Still wondering if we needed four tires on that last pit stop."

"Mirror driving?"

Dad nodded sheepishly. "It's hard not to second-guess yourself. I mean, it's not all bad, so long as you don't get stuck in the past."

"I should've settled for sixth instead of tied for last."

"Kale will probably tell you that, but it's perfect twenty-twenty hindsight." Dad was looking at him. "But when it's your hands on the wheel and you making the split-second decision, it's a gut call." His voice was unusually intense. "I would've made the same call back in the day. I think you can drive, Kyle. If you want to." Then he sighed again and turned back to the screen.

Kyle waited a few beats, but he couldn't come up with the words to keep the conversation going. He was a little breathless.

TWENTY-ONE

"Thought you bought it," Todd said at lunch Monday. Kyle couldn't tell if Todd was glad or sorry to see him in one piece.

"I figured you'd find a way," said Del.

"Were you scared?" asked Nicole.

"Too busy." He remembered what he had said to the flight attendant Saturday night. "Afterward scared spitless."

Nicole honked, and Jesse clapped both fat hands. Even Todd grinned. A couple of the drama kids had wandered over to the band table, and even one of the football players, who said, "Dude, that was running for daylight." He had seen highlights of the race on ESPN.

"I had a great spotter." When he noticed the blank

look on Nicole's face, he said, "Spotter's up on the grandstand roof, sees everything. Tells you on the radio who's coming up on you, what's ahead, when you're clear. She talked me through the wreck."

"She?" said Nicole.

"Red Hoyt's granddaughter," said Kyle, nodding at Del, the only one who would know or care. "It was amazing." He couldn't stop himself. "We were dialed in. Her voice to my hands on the wheel."

"Saw that film," said Jesse. "Holly Hunter and William Hurt in *Broadcast News*. She fed him information while he was on air. He said it was just like sex."

Jesse clapped for himself, but Nicole didn't honk. She doesn't like that, Kyle thought. I do.

Mr. G was energized, waving a sheet of paper overhead like a banner. "I've got mine—do you have yours?"

Kyle looked at Del, who whispered, "Names for the quintet."

This isn't going to work out, thought Kyle. I totally forgot. Didn't think about it at all.

Naturally Mr. G called on him first. "You must have had time to think up names while you were driving around in circles."

Nicole said, "We did it together." She held a sheet of paper out to Kyle. "You want to read them?"

"No, you go ahead."

Jesse clapped his thumb and forefinger. Todd glared.

"Couple of obvious ones," said Nicole. Her hair was pulled back, making her little round face seem bigger. "The Goshen Brass, the Class Brass, Horn Dogs—"

"Hold it." Mr. G rapped his baton on a music stand. "Kyle wasn't involved, was he?" When she looked down, he said, "We have a problem here, people, and we need to address it."

"And mail it," said Jesse.

"Maybe you're the one with the problem," said Nicole.

"Oh?" Mr. G arched an eyebrow. "A little brass warfare?"

"You just want control," she said. Her dark eyes looked fierce to Kyle. She was fighting for him. He felt thrilled and a little scared. For her.

"So it's brass therapy," said Mr. G. His smile was fake.

"Kyle is here," she said. "He comes to practice. He missed one weekend event and one practice because his family needed him. What's the big deal?"

The smile was gone. "Anyone else?"

Kyle checked them out from a corner of one eye. Del was chewing on his lip, not good for a trombone player, and Jesse was jiggling his tuba between big thighs. Todd was tilted back in his chair, smirking at the window. Nicole was staring back at Mr. G.

"Maybe I'm not finished yet," she said.

"Is Kyle finished? That's the question. Is he part of the quintet or not?" Mr. G looked at Kyle. "We need to know if we can depend on you. Can we?"

He felt close to telling Mr. G to sit on his baton, then standing up and walking out. It's what Kris would do. It's what Kris did in the ninth grade when the baseball coach wanted him to choose between being a starting pitcher and racing. He'd already quit football. Why am I comparing myself to Kris?

Besides, Nicole had fought too hard to let her down like that. "I'll do the best I can."

"What does that mean?" said Mr. G.

Good question, thought Kyle. I wish I knew. "Kris should be back in the car next week. I'll be back in my chair."

"I heard should be, not will be," said Mr. G. "What if he isn't?"

"Is this *Law and Order: Band Room*?" said Jesse. When nobody laughed, he pointed a finger at his temple and shot himself. Nobody laughed at that either.

Kyle thought, I don't know. He said, "Hire another driver."

"Why not you?" said Mr. G.

Kyle felt as if the thumbscrew on his music stand

were tightening around his head. "I had a one-race waiver for age. I don't know if they would give me another one."

"What if they do?"

He felt anger bubble up. "Then I'll keep Kris's seat warm as long as it takes, and I'll miss Friday rehearsals so I can make the practices and qualifying before the races."

"Why can't we rehearse around that?" said Del. "A couple of weeks of extra practices during the week, maybe Sunday night, too."

"Works for me," said Jesse.

Nicole glared at Todd until he said, "Sure, count me in."

Mr. G was expressionless. After a while he nodded and said, "Okay. Kyle? Can we count you in?" When Kyle nodded, he said, "We'll do the names next time. Let's perpetrate some sound."

Mr. G looked relieved. Maybe he just needed to show who was in charge, thought Kyle.

He waited until they were out of the building. "Thanks."

"Breaking in a new trumpet player is like training a puppy," she said. "Too much trouble."

"Whatever." But he touched her arm. "No kidding.

Thanks." He thought, I've thanked more girls the past couple of days than in my whole life.

He thought the fierce little eyes softened. Hard to read her. "You going to be able to handle it all?"

That got to him. She understood what he was going through, or at least she was trying to. He wished it were night and she were inviting him back to her house. The words "I don't know" were forming in his head, but before he could decide whether or not to say them, Todd swaggered up. "Am I interrupting something?"

"Yep," she said. Todd shrugged and swaggered off, but the moment was gone. "You busy now?"

"Got to go over the race shop," said Kyle. "Look at the replay, see what happened."

TWENTY-TWO

They watched the race on the big screen in Sir Walter's office, ten of them sprawled on the couches and chairs. Uncle Kale with his bad fat back was stretched out on the carpeted floor. Jackman was holding the DVD player's remote control. Sir Walter was at his desk, autographing eight-by-ten glossy hero cards of himself while he watched. When the tape got to the wreck, everybody perked up. It looked bad from up high. In the car he had seen mostly thick smoke. Then Jimmie's voice cut through the screaming metal. "Go to the wall."

"What took you so long?" said Uncle Kale.

"Couldn't see," said Jimmie.

"Your job." The fat head rose a few inches off the carpet. "Here's where you blew a chance to get him past the nine car. Pause it."

The image stopped, flickered. Through the smoke Kyle could see number 12's nose inches from number 9. He didn't remember that.

"He's blocked," said Jimmie.

"Look at the angle," said Uncle Kale. "Kiss that rear fender, sucker's gone."

Kyle looked around. Jimmie's face was flushed. Dad, Sir Walter, Billy, Jackman, nobody had anything to say. The post-race analysis was Uncle Kale's show.

"Trying to get through the wreck," said Kyle, "not add to it."

"You do what you need to do," said Uncle Kale. "You don't have to react to every bump or block just because they want you to. Sometimes you just grip the wheel a little tighter and hold on. And sometimes you have to bump their tail to show them you're there. You got that, Jimmie?" When she nodded, he said, "Okay, hit play."

Kyle tried to catch Jimmie's eye, smile at her, nod, but her head was down. Uncle Kale and Mr. G, he thought, two control freaks who always need to be right or at least to be standing on top of somebody.

But he was feeling pretty good. It was the first time he had ever watched a video of one of his own races with the entire Hildebrand Racing team. It was like playing a solo.

On-screen, Number 12 was driving slowly under a yellow caution flag. Kyle watched himself hold his line. He was driving steady.

"What you doing wrong here, Kylie?"

He shook his head. He had no idea.

"Why don't you tell him, Jimmie," said Uncle Kale.

"If I knew, I would've told him then," she said. Kyle thought she sounded annoyed. Not the type to take a beating, even from Uncle Kale.

"Anybody?" He hoisted himself to a sitting position and looked around. Even if he was such a genius, why did he have to be so nasty?

It came to Kyle. Or he figured it out. Or he remembered it from one of the thousand dinner table conversations. What else did they ever talk about? "I should've been going side to side, keep the tires warm."

"Bingo," said Uncle Kale. "So why didn't you do it?"

It didn't get much better after that, Kale picking on him and Jimmie. With two laps to go, Kyle just behind the purple Toyota, Slater on his right, Boyd coming up on his left, Uncle Kale said, "Here's the big rookie mistake. You let Slater sucker you in."

Kyle remembered seeing the sudden opening between purple and green and driving into it, feeling triumphant as Slater faded back. He was almost door to door with the purple Toyota when Slater bumped him on the left fender and spun him into the wall. Slater hadn't missed the perfect angle to kiss that rear fender. Sucker's gone. Me.

He remembered the sick feeling when the car stalled. The helplessness as everyone passed him, a few hitting him. Jimmie was screaming at him to go to neutral and turn left. The car sputtered, and Randall Bean tapped him hard enough to get him started again and over the line.

"Rookie luck," said Uncle Kale. "Got a girl and an old man to save your sorry butt."

Sir Walter lifted the stack of signed pictures and tapped them into an even pile. "We're gonna have to send you to charm school, Kale, before the Family Brands people get to hear you."

"If we win," said Uncle Kale, "Family Brands won't care if I talk like one of them comics on HBO."

Everybody laughed at that, even Jimmie.

Uncle Kale clambered to his feet, groaning and punching his back. Lose a hundred pounds, thought Kyle, you won't hurt so much. Did he really say, "The kid was out there to win, and you can't teach that"?

"What time's school out, Kylie?"

"Five thirty."

"So late?"

"Band practice."

"Oh." He dismissed that with a wave. "Need you at Goshen Raceway by three thirty tomorrow for some real practice." Swaying from side to side, he lumbered out of the office and headed to the repair bays.

Dad wouldn't meet his eyes. Have to talk about this at dinner. No more deals?

Jimmie followed him out to the parking lot.

"Don't feel bad," she said. "It's his way. You did good."

I should be trying to make you feel better, he thought. "You did good."

"We did good." She stuck out her hand. It felt just as he'd imagined it, square and strong, but warm. "So what are you gonna do?"

"About what?" He was stalling.

"I'm sure you'll do the right thing," she said, and headed back into the race shop.

He had a flashback of standing in the high-school parking lot with Nicole. You going to be able to handle it all?

TWENTY-THREE

Kyle could hear Mom and Dad arguing downstairs in the kitchen when he crossed the hall to Kris's room. Kris was poking at a racing video game, squinting at the screen like he was having trouble focusing. Without looking up, he said, "Uncle Kale beat up on you?"

"How'd you know?"

"Suck it up. He wouldn't bother if he didn't think . . ." His voice trailed off. Kyle couldn't tell if he had lost the thought or decided to flush it.

"How you feeling?"

"I'm going crazy." His face was pale and puffy.

"Only been a week."

"Nine friggin' days."

"Takes time."

"Doctors don't know squat, and you sure don't." He turned back to his game and slumped in his chair.

"So how you know Jimmie?"

"Who?" On-screen, Kris was crashing.

"Jimmie. Red Hoyt's granddaughter. The redhead?"

"She showed up with Grandpa. She's yours. She goes with the car." There was no energy in his voice.

Dad called them down.

They barely talked through dinner. The Speed Channel was on in the living room, just loud enough to hear familiar names and phrases. Richard Childress's Busch team was bringing up a young driver from the AutoZone West series. Tony Stewart and somebody else's crew chief almost had a fistfight in the garage area before a cup race. A girl was doing okay in the Craftsman Truck series. Usually Dad and Kris would have chewed over that information, but neither of them reacted tonight. Before dessert Kris got up without excusing himself and clomped upstairs with the slow, heavy step of an old man.

"Now what?" said Mom. She sounded very tired.

"Wait, watch. The MRI was good news."

"What about another opinion?" asked Mom.

"So long as there's no bleeding in the brain, no evidence of damage . . ." Dad shrugged and turned to Kyle.

"Kale was a little rough on you."

"His way," said Kyle. He wanted to talk about it, but not in front of Mom.

"Only reason he beat up on you, he thinks you've got possibilities."

"C'mon, Kerry, that's enough," said Mom.

But Kyle wanted to hear more. He felt a flutter in his stomach. He tried to sound casual and sarcastic. "Possibilities for what?"

"He liked what he saw. You were steady, patient, alert. Brave." Dad stopped when Mom jumped up, collected some plates with a clatter, and marched into the kitchen. "You remember he took it personal when you quit racing."

"There was something else I wanted to do. It's my life."

"He just saw wasted talent. He didn't see the school band as a reasonable alternative to racing. Now he's got a second chance with you."

"In his dreams," said Kyle. "I'm not Kris." That just popped out. Part of him wanted to snatch the words back, part of him to let them lie there, examine them. *What do I mean?*

"Of course you're not Kris. You got your own style."

"I'm just keeping his seat warm."

"Remember that," said Mom. She was carrying two open containers of ice cream. "This is temporary."

"This is what Kyle wants to make of it," said Dad.

She put the containers down with a thump. "I really hope you mean that."

"No pressure, Lynda. I promised you."

Uncle Kale thinks I've got possibilities, thought Kyle. Why should I care what old fatback thinks?

After he finished in the bathroom, he checked on Kris. He was lying on top of the bedcovers holding the two Labs. He never did that. He was usually either wrestling with them or ignoring them.

There were messages from Nicole and Del and Mr. G. There was a message from Jackman. He had never gotten a message from Jackman before. He opened it first.

Hey, Kyle, That was some ballsy race. The crews behind you 110 percent.

The J Man.

It was just a little more pressure, he knew, to keep him in the car until Kris was ready. Maybe Uncle Kale put Jackman up to it. But it made him feel good.

Until it made him feel bad.

When classes are over tomorrow, do I go to quintet practice or race practice?

Suddenly he wanted to talk to Jimmie. Would he call her if he had her number? What would he say?

What's the right thing?

He wondered if he would have the dream tonight, running three wide with Dad and Kris.

Suck it up, Kyle—this is your deal.

TWENTY-FOUR

Mr. G called him out of class, a first. Kyle felt nervous walking into the Music Department office, and he didn't feel better when Mr. G came around his desk with a big smile, his hand out. He imagined Mr. G's handshake damp and flabby, but he never found out. Mr. G made a fist and bumped Kyle's fist three times, knuckle to knuckle, and then top and bottom hammers. The rappers weren't even doing that on TV anymore.

Mr. G was wearing Converse sneakers, threadbare jeans, and a Dung Beetle T-shirt. Terminal hip. Grow up.

"Sit down, Kyle." He motioned to one of the two wooden armchairs in front of his desk, the parents' chairs. Mr. G turned the other chair to face Kyle. When they were both sitting, their knees almost touching, Mr. G leaned over to pluck a piece of paper from his desk. It was a printout of the e-mail Kyle had sent last night.

"You say here you're going to miss this week, at the least. You can't be sure when you'll be back. We're preparing for an audition in three weeks we can win only if we're together. What should we do?"

Kyle felt his throat closing up. "Maybe you should find another trumpet."

"As good as you? With your promise? I don't think so." He paused, his brown eyes blinking.

Kyle wondered if he was supposed to react to that. Just hold your line, see what kind of deal he's running.

"You know how passionate I am about arts education, especially in a climate where it's being cut all over the place. The quintet has been a special dream of mine, and when the Brooklyn Brass invited us to join them, I thought my dreams were finally coming true. I should have realized that it simply wasn't that important to everyone."

"It's important to me." He was immediately sorry he had reacted, but it was too late. He hoped it wouldn't turn out as badly as letting Slater sucker him into the hole.

"Really?" Mr. G drew the word out.

And sometimes you have to bump their tail to show

them you're there. "I know you wouldn't want me to let my family down."

Mr. G's blinking slowed down. He felt that, thought Kyle. Don't get overconfident now. "I don't want to quit the quintet. I want to make this all work."

"So do I," said Mr. G. "Show me how we can do it without letting down Jesse and Todd and Del and Nicole. And the Brooklyn Brass. And the idea that arts are as important as sports."

Suckered in again, he thought. He was in a spin, heading for the wall. Hang on. "I'll make as many practices as I can until my brother comes back."

They sat still, staring at each other until Mr. G stood up, picked up his baton, and circled his desk, tapping books, his computer, CDs. "What does Kyle Hildebrand want, really want—where does he want to be in a year, five years?" He whirled and jabbed the baton at Kyle.

"I don't know."

"That feels real." Mr. G flipped the baton, caught it, spun it between his fingers. "But it doesn't answer our problem. Racing is going to take more and more of your time just when the quintet is going to require more and more of your time."

He felt small, helpless. "I'll do the best I can."

"I'm going to keep your seat . . . warm," said Mr. G. "For a week, maybe two if I can. Then you'll have to compete to get it back. Fair?"

Kyle nodded. He wanted to get out of the office.

Mr. G waved him out. "Drive safely."

Out in the hall, he thought, It's Uncle Kale's possibilities against Mr. G's promise. There's a race. Me against me.

TWENTY-FIVE

Goshen Raceway needed a paint job. For starters. The metal fences were sagging, and there were cracks in the dingy white concrete walls. The wooden grandstand was splintery, and the quarter-mile oval track was still littered with Saturday night's marbles, the little black balls of rubber left by sling cars driven by weekend wannabes who would never race anywhere else.

Looking down at the track from a hill behind the chain-link fence that circled the raceway, Kyle felt sad for its shabbiness. It had been years since the family had had serious money to pour into it. They needed to rent it out for concerts and demolition derbies and monster truck races just to pay the bills. He remembered when it was bright and shiny, the pride he'd felt standing up here after one of his quarter-midget races, seeing the arch of the front gate with its deep-blue sign, Home of the Hildebrands. Great-grandpa Fred had built the track, and Grandpa Walter had made it the biggest attraction in the county. Sections of the grandstand were named for Fred and Walter and Kerry and Kris. Once he had wanted people sitting under his name too. But that seemed like a long time ago, before Dad finally retired and Kris moved on to the bigger tracks in Monroe, Charlotte, and Richmond.

That was when the track started closing in on him, squeezing the air out of his chest. People started looking at him as the next Kris and treating him as if he had no more choices in his life but to follow his brother, following Dad and Sir Walter.

He wondered if that was what Uncle Ken had felt, no choices but to follow in Sir Walter's long blue shadow. Master Sergeant Kenton Hildebrand, the one who got away. Like to meet him again someday.

In the garage area below, a motor turned over. He spotted the Hildebrand hauler. Better get down there.

Dad, Uncle Kale, and Billy were working on number 12. They'd be taking the car out soon.

Dad spotted him. "New setup."

"Get your suit on," said Uncle Kale.

Billy gave him a smile and a wave. "Sorry I wimped on you Saturday."

"He did just fine," snapped Uncle Kale.

Kyle lifted his duffel bag out of the Camaro's trunk. He found a quiet corner and changed into his old fire suit. There were logos on it from Billy's brother's auto body shop, Aunt Susan's haircutter franchise, and Del's family's restaurant. The suit was snug across the chest, and the pants didn't cover his ankles. Been a while.

He was pulling on his shoes when his cell phone vibrated. "Where are you?" said Nicole.

"At the track. I worked out a deal with Mr. G."

"He's got Justin in your chair." She sounded pissed. "Was that part of the deal?"

"I didn't think right away." Justin was a sophomore, an okay trumpet. "What did he say?"

"He said Justin was keeping your seat warm as long as you were keeping your brother's seat warm."

Uncle Kale hollered, "Let's go, Kylie."

"Got to go. Call you tonight."

"What should we do?"

He was suddenly mad at her. Why is that my problem, too? "Perpetrate some sound." He snapped the cell shut.

Number 12 was the only car testing. Kyle wondered if Dad had told them to keep the track clear.

The new springs and shock setup was stiffer, giving the car more forward bite off the turns. On the third lap he opened the throttle, and Uncle Kale's voice was in his head. "Okay, now let's learn how to turn left."

He had to tighten his grip on the wheel. He thought of Justin sitting in his chair next to Nicole, warming up on "Pavane for a Dead Princess." "What?"

"You're driving too deep into the turn. You're over-heating the brakes, I can smell them from the pit."

"Float," said Dad. "Try to float in, Kyle, and turn sooner."

Float. That was what they never could get Kris to do. Kris didn't have to. He could drive his own way and win. What am I doing here?

On the next turn he eased off the gas and swung left earlier than he usually did, rotating off the wall. The car was bad fast.

"That's better," said Dad. He sounded happy.

Nothing from Uncle Kale.

He floated in again on the next two turns before he heard Uncle Kale's grunt. "Okay. Eight more like that and you can come in."

TWENTY-SIX

Jackman showed up for dessert. Kyle was glad to see him. Big and loud, he changed the mood in the dining room. He rubbed his knuckles across Kyle's scalp. "Peyton's band's playing at Lobo. Wanna come?"

"School night." He liked being asked, but he was exhausted and way behind on homework. He needed to call Nicole.

"Jimmie'll be there," said Jackman. "Good-bye party."

"She leaving?"

Kris picked up his tone and mimicked it. "She leaving? Who will whisper in my ear?"

They laughed harder than the line was worth, happy to see Kris part of the conversation. He was looking better, color in his face, the puffiness gone. He had new pills for the headaches and the nausea. The doctors wouldn't clear him for Saturday, but it shouldn't be long now.

"How come?"

"She and Kale had some words," said Jackman. "You know Kale."

"Not exactly a people person," said Mom dryly. Dad shot her a look.

"Not exactly a person," said Kris. Mom laughed.

"I thought Grandpa signed her on," said Kyle. He felt a stab of loss.

"He's out of town," said Dad. "Besides, she quit. She wasn't fired. Tried to talk to her, but her mind was set."

"Kale got on her and she wouldn't take it," said Jackman.

"Why should she?" said Mom.

"That's his way," said Jackman. "Crew chief's like a football coach. Not a democracy. Only one hand on the wheel."

"Maybe I will come out with you guys," said Kyle.

Lobo was out on the highway toward Charlotte, the kind of boots bar Kyle had never been comfortable in. He was glad to walk in with Jackman, who could clear a path just by shrugging his shoulders, and Kris, who seemed to know everybody. Or at least they knew him. When the owner spotted them, he had a table set up near the stage. Jackman ordered a beer. Kris popped a pill and ordered a Jump. Kyle said, "Make it two."

"Stuff's the worst," said Kris. "But that's the deal. In public."

"Better with rum," said Kyle. "Call it Rump."

That got a laugh. Jackman said, "Better get back fast, Kris—this rookie'll steal your car."

"Gonna be two cars," said Kris. "For starters."

"Who says?" said Kyle.

"All the big-time teams have at least three, and Family Brands wants to be big time," said Jackman. "Kerry and Sir Walter meeting with the suits tomorrow."

Kris said, "The Hildebrand Boys, running one, two."

"Hope you'll be happy number two," said Kyle. He was feeling up. When was the last time he'd been out alone with Kris and Jackman? Ever?

Jackman howled and knuckled Kyle. Kris laughed, but not so hard. "Gonna need a second crew chief," Kris said. "That why you're kissing Kyle's ass, Jackoff?"

Jackman said, "Two new crew chiefs, both reporting to Kale as director of operations. That's how the big teams do it."

"Teammates competing against each other," said Kyle.

"It can work," said Jackman, "depending on the drivers and the director."

"The people person," said Kris. "Why's Mom so down on Uncle Kale?"

Because of me, Kyle thought.

The cowgirl band onstage was whiney. No wonder the boyfriends in their songs had left them. But the lead singer was pretty, and she was beaming her voice directly to Kris. Jackman had his eye on the rhythm guitarist, a big-busted girl who could play a little. Kyle thought, Damn, I never called Nicole. Maybe go outside for a minute.

"Hey, guys." Jimmie sat down. She seemed pleased to see Kyle. Her red hair was loose and she was wearing lipstick. A low-cut red blouse was tucked into black jeans. She looked good.

The cowgirl band finished, and the band they'd come to see clomped onstage and started warming up. They spotted Kris and Jackman and made them stand and wave to the crowd. Jackman pulled Kyle up with them. Drinks they hadn't ordered appeared on the table, along with bowls of nachos and dip. The two cowgirl guitarists pulled up chairs.

Jackman leaned over to Kyle and said, "You think Dale Jr.'s got it better than this?"

The band was okay, Wilco wannabes, Kyle thought, and Peyton, the tire-carrier drummer, was usually on beat and loud enough to make talking impossible. Jackman got into it, stomping and clapping. Kris looked like he was going into a trance. Mom and Dad had liked the idea of him getting out of the house with Jackman, whom they trusted to watch over him, but Kyle wondered how clear his mind was. Kris was almost always focused, but now he seemed a little drifty. Was he having trouble concentrating?

After a little while Kyle couldn't stay with the music. It just wasn't good enough. He kept sneaking glances at Jimmie. He thought she was pretending to be interested, but her eyes seemed faraway.

At the break, Jimmie said, "I better go."

Jackman and Kris promised to stay in touch. They had their hands full of cowgirl.

Kyle said, "Can I ride back with you?"

"Long as I drive."

She had an old black Mustang she handled like a racer. They talked about her car for a few minutes, and when the conversation lagged, Kyle asked, "What did you think of the band?"

She laughed. "I'd call them a real garage band."

"Should've stayed in the garage." Now he felt comfortable enough to ask, "So what are you going to do?"

"Don't know yet."

"What did my grandpa say?"

"I just left him a message I had to go."

"You're letting Kale run you off."

"It wasn't going to work out."

"I really want you spotting for me."

"Billy's feeling better—it'll be okay."

"No, I want you." He was surprised at the intensity in his voice.

She was too. It took her a moment to say, "I can't go back. I said some things."

"What if he asks you back?"

"Yeah, right."

"What if he begs you to come back? I'm serious."

In the light of an oncoming truck, he saw her face. She was smiling. "You are serious. Begs me? On bended knee?"

"No bended knee. Kale wouldn't be able to get up again."

They kept laughing all the way back to Hildebrand Hill. She pulled up outside his house. "Look, Kyle, I really appreciate this, but it's just not going to work out. He and I are—"

He held up his hand the way his parents did to each other. "Give me a day, okay? It's my turn to spot for you, get you through the wreck."

Her face softened. "You got a plan?"

"I do," he lied. "Don't leave till you hear from me. Okay?"

It seemed to take a long time for her to say, "Okay." She wrote her cell number on the back of an old garage-area pass.

TWENTY-SEVEN

He woke up remembering that he hadn't called Nicole, but he couldn't remember what he planned to say to her. He thought of Jimmie. You got a plan? Start with Dad. Then he remembered that Dad was meeting with Grandpa and the suits about a second car.

On the way downstairs, he peeked into Kris's room. The bed hadn't been slept in. He wondered if Kris and Jackman had scored with the cowgirls, if life was shifting back to normal.

Mom was in the kitchen cooking scrambled eggs and bacon. "You need a good breakfast today."

"How come?" He checked his watch. Have to eat fast.

"Intuition." She was standing at the stove, her back to him. "You're only seventeen years old, Kyle. You're a work in progress. You're still young enough to think you can do it all. Don't let them take that away from you."

She popped whole wheat bread out of the toaster and brought his plate to the table. He started eating. It all tasted dry, overdone. "'S good." Had to say something.

She sat down across the table. She looked tired. He wondered if she had been up late arguing with Dad again. "Keep your options open. Don't let anybody limit your choices."

He felt sorry for her. She had to talk in code, try to support him without being disloyal to Dad or the family. He wished he knew how to tell her he understood. Hildebrands don't know how to say things like that, he thought.

"Kris seems a lot better," he said. "He'll be back soon."

"Don't count on that to get you off the hook," she said.

"What do you mean?"

"Two cars. Then three cars."

"Maybe I'll want to drive one."

"Maybe."

"And maybe"—he imagined a long note on the trumpet, fingers moving—"I'll pull an Uncle Ken."

Her head jerked as if he had slapped her. After she caught her breath, she said, "You're not joining the army."

"No, I just meant, you know, make my own choices."

She looked sad. "I liked Kenny a lot. The army was the only way he could break free. It's different for you. College. Maybe music conservatory. I hope. What made you think of him?"

"His name's been coming up."

She nodded. "If Kenny had stayed, your dad might have finished school, become an engineer. But he didn't think he had a choice." Her eyes looked faraway.

On the way out, he kissed the top of her head. Hadn't done that in a long time. "Gonna be okay, Mom."

She grabbed him and hugged him hard. "You've always been such a good boy, such a responsible boy. Don't let them use that against you."

Nobody from quintet was in any of his Wednesday classes, and he went outside for lunch. He ditched his last period class to retrieve his trumpet from the band room, figuring the room would be empty this time of day. He was at his locker before he noticed Jesse in a corner, adjusting a tuba valve.

"Hey. Missed you yesterday. The new kid's lame."

"I'll be back." He fitted the trumpet, the mute, some music, and the soft gig bag into the hard case. "Try to practice some."

"Saw that film. *Genevieve*. Car racing. Dinah Sheridan, Kenneth More, and Kay Kendall's got this hilarious trumpet solo—"

He felt a flash of anger and slammed the locker shut. "Get a life."

He was almost at the door when he heard Jesse say, "Everybody's busting your balls, huh?" Jesse's voice sounded sympathetic. When he turned, he saw the big dark moon face looked sympathetic, too.

"Kinda."

"Listen, man, we understand. Nobody thinks you're bailing on us. Everybody knows family can put your Johnson in a clamp."

He nodded.

"You coming to Mr. G's dinner party?"

"Didn't know about it."

"Read your e-mails. Nicole's been trying to reach you. It's Sunday night at his house. Be there, Kyle. You have friends."

He wondered if he could talk to Jesse, but what would he say? He heard voices outside in the hall and remembered he wanted to get out before Nicole showed up for practice. "Thanks, Jesse." That didn't seem enough, but it was the best he could do.

Jackman had Kris on the weight machines in the gym when Kyle got to the race shop. He watched them through the glass wall. Kris was sweating and slow, but he was lifting steadily. Jackman hovered over him. They stopped and waved Kyle in.

"I could put you on a program too," said Jackman.

"For one week?"

Jackman and Kris exchanged glances. Kris said, "Family Brands signed off on a new car right away, call it number twelve A. The plan is, number twelve is gonna move up to Busch, maybe even this season, and then to cup."

"This all happen today?" said Kyle. He felt a cold hard lump forming in his stomach.

"Nailed today. But they been talking about it since Family Brands came around. Where you been?"

"So even when you're back . . ." Kyle let the sentence trail. He felt stupid. Didn't matter if he had a plan or not. They had a plan.

"You're the man, man," said Jackman.

"What about the age waiver?" Kyle felt as though he were grabbing for a life preserver in a storm. "It was only for one—"

"Family Brands gets what it wants," said Kris.

"About time," said Uncle Kale, rapping on the gym's glass door. "Go sit in the car."

"We got to talk," said Kyle.

"I need you sitting in the car while we tweak the engine." Uncle Kale turned and started walking away.

"We can talk later."

"Now," said Kyle.

"Go, bro," said Kris.

Uncle Kale turned slowly. "Lots to do. Talk fast."

"I want Jimmie back spotting for me."

"She quit."

"Get her back." He liked the sound of his voice. He thought of a whip snapping.

"Do her on your own time—this is a race team."

"Better keep your drivers happy, Uncle Kale." Kris cackled.

Kyle dug his cell phone out of his jeans. "I got her number."

"She's disruptive. I don't want her around."

"I want her around. Family Brands wants her around. Sir Walter wants her around."

Uncle Kale's small eyes were hot as he watched Kyle dial a number with a quivering thumb. He took Kyle's cell and raised it to his ear without ever taking his eyes off Kyle's face.

"It's Kale. I want you at the shop. Now." He snapped the phone shut and tossed it to Kyle. He was around the corner before Jackman and Kris whooped and high-fived. Kyle felt light-headed and scared. He had won.

What had he won? And what had he sacrificed for the victory?

TWENTY-EIGHT

They worked on the new setup the rest of the week and took it out twice more on the Goshen track. At first Kyle didn't understand why Uncle Kale insisted he sit in the car while they tweaked the engine, wondered if it was just another case of him exerting control, maybe punishment for making him ask Jimmie back. But Uncle Kale never mentioned Jimmie, just yelled over the engine noise for Kyle to stay alert, to feel the vibrations. At first Kyle sat in the car, hot and bored, thinking about the trumpet in its case under his bed, wondering when he would play it again.

But once he began to concentrate on feeling the differences in vibrations, on hearing the differences in sounds, time moved more quickly. The harder he concentrated, the more he heard the music of the car, the shifts in pitch and rhythm as rubber and metal and plastic reacted to acceleration, to the angle of a turn, to weather.

Out on the track he became an interpreter of the car's music, radioing back reports on the motor, the chassis, the tires, the springs, as he floated into the turns and opened up on the straightaways. Mostly Uncle Kale just grunted at what he had to say, but once when he reported a softness in the shocks and again when he felt a faint grind in the brakes, Uncle Kale called him back into the pits, where he and Billy were waiting with tools in their hands like surgeons in the ER. Those times Uncle Kale sent him back out again with an almost pleasant "Keep it up." Kyle couldn't help smiling. He began to understand that Uncle Kale was trying to turn him into a part of the machine, the human piece of the car. Or the monkey in the rocket.

He saw Jimmie from a distance in the race shop, working with the fabricators bending a sheet of metal into a car roof. They were building 12A. Her face was flushed. She looked happy. He was thinking about what he would say to her when Jackman grabbed his arm and pulled him into the gym. He seemed to know what he was doing. He already had a checklist for Kyle. Cardiovascular and stretching exercises every day, different weight machines on different days.

"Gotta build stamina," said Jackman. "Drivers start making mistakes at the end of a race because they're tired. Sitting for a couple of hours takes more out of you than you'd think."

"What do you think I do at band?"

"At band nobody's trying to spin you into the wall," said Jackman.

"You'd be surprised."

He saw Nicole at lunch on Thursday. She was sitting at the band table between Todd and the new trumpet, Justin. Kyle waved at her and she waved back, no expression on her face. That was it. He thought about going over, but there were no seats close to her. He'd be at the other end with the freshman horns.

He sat with Billy's grandson at a gearhead table. They knew all about the testing at Goshen and the second car. They treated him the way he'd seen Kris treated, everybody with questions but acting supercool to disguise their respect for a real driver. It was okay.

He ate dinner alone with Mom Thursday night. Dad was taking meetings in Atlanta with Sir Walter and the suits. Kris was back in the apartment with Jackman. The doctors were pretty sure he could drive in another week.

"Ain't nobody here but us chickens." Mom hummed the old blues song as she served salmon and a salad. Kyle remembered playing it years ago with her.

"Dad called," she said. "They're staying in Atlanta overnight. He said he'll meet you in Monroe tomorrow."

"You going?"

"Too many lessons. It's recital season. You get a chance to practice at all?"

"Only on the steering wheel." He thought it was a good line, something to lighten the mood, but she didn't even smile. "Maybe we can play after dinner."

That got a smile. "Be nice. What are you playing for Mr. Sievers?"

"Some Vizzutti caprices . . ."

"They're hard," she said.

". . . and some Leonard Bernstein for fun. He was annoyed I didn't come Saturday."

"He should get in line." She shook her head. "Music can slip away from you." They ate in silence for a while. He imagined Mom was thinking about herself. She had met Dad in college. She was a music major. After he quit to race in Uncle Ken's place, she started going to the track to watch him, and then eventually she quit college too, and they got married and had kids.

Mom said, "I heard you made Kale take Jimmie back."

"She does a good job."

"She got you through the wreck—we're all grateful for that." Mom got up and came back to the table with a bottle of white wine and a glass. "Did you want to keep her as your spotter?"

"Sure."

"You went up against Uncle Kale just for one or two races."

He sensed where she was going and tried to change the direction. "She knows her way around a car. They need more people."

"Of course they do." She poured herself a glass. "What did they say to you about the second car?"

He'd taken the wrong direction. Or she was just too slick for him. "They're building it. They're interviewing drivers."

"I'm sure they'd like to keep it in the family."

"Nobody asked me."

"Did you tell them no?"

"I said nobody asked me."

"Sweetie," she said, "they've been asking you all your life."

"I haven't made any decisions yet."

"You've been thinking about it?"

"Sure."

"So you understand that they want you in the second

car, and this business about just keeping Kris's seat warm is so much crap." She never used language like that. "Hey, I went along with it, too. I should have put my foot down when they wanted you to spot for Kris."

"Maybe he'd still be driving if I hadn't called the sling." It was the first time it had come out as a fully formed thought.

She raised her glass. "Take your guilt trips by yourself." She took a long sip. "Kris would have done it without you and probably gotten wrecked."

"You think so?" He felt grateful.

She shrugged. "I don't really know. But that's what Uncle Kale and your dad think."

"They never said that to me."

"Why would they? Go get your trumpet."

He took his time. He wanted to think about that. Why would they? Why wouldn't they want him to feel guilty, to feel he had to keep Kris's seat warm after helping knock him out of it? Everybody's got their own agenda in this family. I gotta get one too.

He checked his e-mail. Mr. G and Jesse and Del and Nicole all reminding him about the Sunday dinner. Funky casual, whatever that meant. I want to go.

When he got downstairs, Mom was at the keyboard, her wineglass on the piano. She flashed a bright, forced smile. "What's your pleasure, treasure?"

He figured it would be a bluesy night. He remembered one of their old routines and tried to match her mood. "Think you can play Dizzy?'

"Only way I can play, pal."

"'Autumn Leaves'?" He knew she loved that. She had found an old recording of Oscar Peterson on piano and Dizzy Gillespie on trumpet, and they had tried to match it. Never came close, of course, but it was one of their best.

"Too sad. Too much loss. How about 'Jumpin' at the Woodside'?"

"Let's see what you got, lady."

They wailed.

TWENTY-NINE

The crew went nuts when the red, green, and deep-blue number 12 Family Brands Ford qualified in fifth place for the Prince Pizza 250, the best pole position the car had won all season. They hugged Kyle and pounded one another and jumped on Jackman's back. It was proof that all their hard work had paid off, the new setup worked, they had created a speedier machine. And the rookie could drive.

They were standing outside the Family Brands hospitality tent when the final qualifying numbers flickered on the scoreboard. Dad punched Uncle Kale's big chest, and Sir Walter grabbed both their heads and pretended to knock them together. A Family Brands video crew shot them. Winik and the other executives high-fived.

Uncle Kale turned to Kyle and said, "Up to you now."

Later he wished he had thought faster and said something like It's the car, stupid. But he was caught up in the excitement of being so close to the front. Can I hold that lead? Kris won with cars that didn't even qualify in the top twenty, he was that good. I'm not Kris. Maybe that was what Uncle Kale was really saying. It's your race to lose, Kylie.

Uncle Kale signaled to the crew and lumbered off to the garage area. Jackman and the crew fell into line behind Kale like kids on a field trip. Follow the leader.

"Ready to rock, li'l bro?" Kris knuckled his head. He almost looked like himself. You'd have to know him well, Kyle thought, to notice the fatigue in his face. Kris still winced at bright lights or sudden loud noises, but he was standing straight and the quick grin was back. So was the mischief. When two Family Brands guests, a couple of twenty-somethings whose boobs were jumping out of their halter tops, came over for autographs, Kris wrote, "From Kyle Hildebrand, little brother of the future king." They squealed and kissed him.

"How about kissing Kyle?" said Kris, pointing to Kyle. "Even ugly guys need love."

They lunged for Kyle, but Dad pulled him away. "Gotta go. Time enough for that up the road."

But this could be the end of the road, Kyle thought.

The last race. Family Brands had had no trouble extending his exemption for this race, but could they really get a waiver for the rest of this season? He wouldn't be eighteen until the start of next season, in the middle of his senior year.

At the garage Uncle Kale and Jackman were fussing with a rag on the engine. If that's all they can think of to do, Kyle thought, number 12 is ready. It's up to me now.

"You stay in the top five," said Uncle Kale, "everybody's happy and you've got yourself a ride in—"

"Kale." Dad had the stop sign up.

"One race at a time." Uncle Kale's beady eyes swept around until they found Jimmie. "Get upstairs. Stay alert. Remember, this is no talk show."

Jimmie nodded at Uncle Kale and pumped a fist at Kyle. She looked too wound up to let Uncle Kale's tone get to her. She hurried off to the grandstand.

"You could tap that ass," said Kris, watching her go.

"Yeah, right," said Kyle. He wanted to think about that, but not now.

It felt different this time, like number 12 was his car, not a loaner from Kris. It had been rebuilt, and he had qualified in it.

People treated him differently—heartier handshakes

from the suits, more attention from the fans, nods at the drivers' meeting. Getting through the wreck had earned him some respect.

Ruff brushed past him without a word, but Gary Nagle said to him and Dad, "Nothing personal, what I said last week," and Dad answered, "Didn't take it personal," and they shook hands. Elliott Slater gave Kyle a hard look. Reminded Kyle of boxing matches on ESPN Classic where old-timey fighters try to stare down each other. Kyle grinned back, and Slater walked away.

Boyd was friendly. Must be angling for a seat in the new car, Kyle thought. "Got sponsorship for this race," said Boyd. "New FM station. Might sign for the season."

"Good luck," said Dad.

"Be better if I was a minority," said Boyd, tilting his head toward the only black face in the room. "Walks in with an army sponsorship."

"He was a real good open-wheel driver," said Dad. "Lloyd Rogers. Experienced."

"He's here on a diversity program," said Boyd.

"Still got to drive," said Kyle.

"See if he can take the bangin'." Boyd swaggered away.

When they ran into Randall Bean, Kyle thanked him for the push.

"Ask your dad how many times I got a push from him

or Sir Walter," he said. "Glad I was there. You could be a good one."

Dad thanked him and shook his hand. On the way back to the garage, Dad said, "Randall's a good judge of talent."

Kyle felt Kris's eyes on him as he climbed into the car. Must look feeble to him, he thought, one leg at a time through the window, then wriggling down into the seat. He wondered if Kris would still be able to do his famous jackknife into the car.

C'mon, focus.

He adjusted himself into the seat and mounted the steering wheel. Uncle Kale and Jackman slipped his helmet on and tightened his seat belts and his head-and-neck restraint. He tested the radio. Jackman looped the straw from the water sack hanging behind the seat. No more cups at the end of a pole. They had installed state-of-the-art cold drink systems in both cars.

"Remember to bite down for water, Kylie," said Uncle Kale.

"Kyle," said Kyle. "Name is Kyle."

"Sure." said Uncle Kale. He didn't seem offended, didn't really seem to care. Should have done this a long time ago. But he wouldn't listen until I was a racer.

He had never driven a car so ready to run. Number 12 felt like a stallion. On the parade lap the engine throbbed with complaint at being held back. He needed to keep a foot on the brake even when he eased up on the gas. The wheel pulled at his arms. Let's go!

He was ready to go too.

When the green flag came down, the car behind him tried to nose inside and pass, but Kyle didn't give an inch. It was Slater. The green Ford fell back into sixth place.

"That's it," said Uncle Kale. "Hold your line, Kyle."

The early laps were brisk but steady. The front row cars held their places and no one got too aggressive. Gary was leading and Ruff was in third place. They had qualified ahead of Kyle, but he wasn't convinced their cars were really faster in the long haul. Just concentrate on keeping your position, he reminded himself. But number 12 felt strong enough to go the distance, maybe even move up.

Take it easy—you're just here to keep Kris's seat warm. This could be your last race.

What was Uncle Kale starting to say when Dad shut him down? Tease him with a shot at driving 12A? Forget it. Two weeks from now, when number 12 and number 12A are both racing at Lowe's Motor Speedway in Charlotte, this Hildebrand is going to be blowing the trumpet. Hire Boyd. Hire Mr. Diversity.

"Purple Toyota coming up." It was the first he had

heard Jimmie's voice this race.

He sneaked a peek. A flash of purple three or four cars behind. Lloyd Rogers had worked his way into the top ten. Kyle remembered being briefly boxed between Slater and Rogers last week. Rogers came out of nowhere last week and left me for dead, and he's coming back up today.

Not going to pass me this time, Rogers.

Slater was blocking Rogers at the tail end of the front runners. Boyd was behind Rogers, yellow and red lightning bolts painted on his white car along with the FM station's call letters and numbers.

Time to move up? Won't be long now, Kyle thought, before the pack starts pushing forward, putting pressure on the front-runners.

"Hold your line," said Uncle Kale, reading his mind.

THIRTY

He was excited but he wasn't jittery, channeling the energy into keeping control of the car and staying alert. He was relaxed enough to let his eyes flick around, check the mirror, check the windows, scope the front-runners through the windshield. Like being in the quintet, he thought. You concentrate on your part, the music, the fingering, the breath, but you keep listening to the others, be part of the whole, avoid losing the tempo, steer away from collisions of sound. You need to visualize your part in the puzzle in both places, and here you have to know where the other cars are, and you have to let your car talk to you: the reassuring thumping of the engine, the whine of the gears, the squeal of metal tortured by the wrenching left turns and the air rushing past. The music of the cars as beautiful as the music of the horns.

Uncle Kale called him in for gas and tires.

He was aware of all the sound and movement around him, Jackman shouting orders to the crew, Peyton carrying away the old tire, then checking the front grill for bits of rubber, the gas man going for the second can while the catch-can man held the first one in place. Fourteen seconds and they were all done and he was driving back onto the track.

It was a boat race, lap after lap after lap, fast but boring as the front-runners held their positions. No crashes. There was shifting in the Pack and in the Clot, but that had nothing to do with him. Number 9, the car Uncle Kale had criticized him for not bumping into the wall in the last race, leaked oil, and the caution flag came out until it was cleaned up, and then the parade continued. He fought to keep his mind on the race, checking the lap counter on the scoreboard, forty-nine to go, briefly letting his mind split-screen: Why not bring Nicole to a race, maybe with Del to keep her company and explain what was happening, so she could understand me better.

"Slater's gonna bump," yelled Jimmie.

It was just enough warning to tighten his grip on the wheel and prepare his feet to accelerate or brake or both before the green Ford tapped him. Kyle held on, steered into the spin and out in time to block Slater from passing inside.

Nice try, dingleberry.

The pace picked up. Ruff moved into second place, half a length behind Gary. In the mirror Kyle saw the purple Toyota make a bold sweeping pass that brought it outside Boyd's lightning-bolt white Pontiac. They were running door to door behind Slater.

He tried to imagine what might happen next.

Boyd and Rogers were outsiders at this track, and for all Boyd's yap about diversity drivers, he might team up with Rogers for a couple of laps, at least to get them past Slater. They might be able to pull an old trick. Boyd and Rogers would drive two abreast behind Slater, maybe even tapping him. Then they would split, Boyd low to the left, Rogers high to the right. Slater would go crazy weaving left and right to keep them from passing. Sooner or later, if Boyd and Rogers kept working together, one of them would find a hole big enough to drive into. He would either blast past Slater or ride door to door with him. Then he would team up with Slater to start the process again.

Against me.

Got to think this through. If Rogers is the one makes it, Slater will never team up with him, a young open-wheeler

179

he can't trust and knows nothing about. If Boyd makes it, Slater might just give it a shot, figuring he's smarter than Boyd and can ditch him once they knock me off and start fighting for a top-five spot.

"Don't drift," snapped Uncle Kale. "Keep your eyes peeled."

Up ahead the leaders were about to lap Randall. Poor old guy never had the equipment to do much. Hey, don't feel sorry for him, he's a survivor, he's out here when most guys his age are watching races. Keep Randall in mind—he can be helpful again.

"Purple Toyota and white lightning," said Jimmie. "Two on Slater."

He felt piss splatter out and dry on his thigh. The stink disappeared in the gas fumes. His head began to ache from the carbon monoxide buildup.

"Slater bumping," said Jimmie. She sounded psyched.

"No play by play," said Uncle Kale.

In the rearview he saw Slater's green Ford lurch forward. He felt a slight touch and tapped the gas, bringing himself to the fourth-place car. The green Ford lurched again but didn't reach him this time. Slater was tough, holding his line.

For two laps Kyle watched Slater duel Rogers and Boyd in his rearview mirror. Slater was good; he blocked them both. Then the ninth-place car, a blue

Chevy, moved in between Boyd and Rogers, and they ran three wide for two more laps until one of them bumped Slater toward the wall and Boyd swooped under Slater and passed him.

Now it was Boyd on his tail, with Slater, Rogers, and the blue Chevy bumping and rubbing behind. Those three would never get untangled in time. Just have to worry about Boyd.

Twenty laps to go.

Gary and Ruff were trading the lead, the third-place car right behind them. Never break into that little clique. But the car ahead in fourth place, a black-and-yellow Dodge, seemed a little loose. Fourth place would be sweet.

Don't risk it. Concentrate on holding fifth, blocking Boyd.

"Ten laps," said Uncle Kale. "Just hold your line."

Just hold your lardass. I'm going to do what I want. Maybe I'll try to blast my way to the front, or maybe I'll let the car slide back, come in, say, twentieth, and then you can hire Boyd or Lloyd Rogers or even Randall Bean to drive 12A.

But it would be Dad the Family Brands suits would go for, he thought, father and son Hildebrands if they couldn't get the brothers. Dad shouldn't be driving. Well, he's a big boy now, he can make that decision.

In this family nobody makes his own decision.

Except me.

"Boyd coming up outside," said Jimmie.

Perfect. Let Boyd take fifth place, then Slater and Rogers can pass me, just keep dropping back and back and back into the Pack, then into the Clot, then waiting to get lapped with my old friend Randall. Finish last with Randall. Been there, done that.

I'm going to hold my line, Uncle Kale. You were wrong—the kid wasn't out there to win, he was out there to do the right thing, and now he's done it and he's going back to his own life. I'm a trumpet player. I'm not going to have to pull a Ken to break free.

The fourth-place black-and-yellow Dodge was getting looser, its rear end sliding up to the wall. If I move fast to get behind him, it'll look like I'm blocking Boyd, who'll try to pass me on the left, but I'll drop down fast to block him on the inside, and Boyd, dummy that he is, will swoop around me and slam into the Dodge and I'll be fourth.

But my timing will have to be perfect, or I'll slam into the Dodge or Boyd into me and I can't see the Dodge in front and Boyd behind at the same time. . . .

Jimmie knew. "Now," she yelled.

Kyle wrenched the wheel to the right, and when she again yelled, "Now," he swerved left and matted the gas, shooting free, seeing only a splash of color in his rearview as Boyd hit the Dodge.

"Clear," yelled Jimmie.

He swept past the spinning tangle of yellow-and-black and yellow-and-red just as the yellow caution flag came down.

Kyle was in fourth place when the race ended a few minutes later, under a yellow flag.

Family Brands uniforms swarmed around the car as he drove into the garage area. Jackman pulled him out of the car. Peyton poured Jump on his head. The rest of the crew were hoisting him on their shoulders. Dad and Sir Walter and the suits were tossing Family Brands packages at the fans. Jimmie was pushing through the crowd toward him. How had she gotten down so fast?

"You scumbag!" Boyd was running toward him, fists balled, his crew behind him. One of them had a tire iron and lunged at number 12. He got in one good shot on the hood before Jackman grabbed him around the waist and wrestled him down.

Kris and the Hildebrand crew rushed out to meet Boyd's crew.

Kyle felt numb. As Boyd reached him, he brought up his fists. They felt heavy.

A wall slid in front of him and Boyd slammed into it.

"Dare you touch my driver," roared Uncle Kale.

He had Boyd by the throat, up in the air, when the cops arrived.

THIRTY-ONE

Standing with Kris on Grandpa's enormous wrap-around porch, Kyle remembered their races, the ones that always ended with him in the flower bed. The day he climbed back up the stairs with a garden rake and whacked Kris across the chest as he skateboarded past was the last day they raced around the porch. Kyle was eight, he thought, Kris ten and already a two-time quarter-midget champ.

"You never beat me." Kris must have been having the same thought.

"But I whipped your ass once."

"You needed a shovel. Blindsided me."

"A rake. You saw it coming."

"Whatever." He threw an arm over Kyle's shoulder.

"Man, was I proud of you yesterday."

"A monkey could've driven that car. . . ."

"The way you stood up to Boyd."

I think I just froze, thought Kyle. "Never saw Uncle Kale move so fast."

"When it comes to the family or the car, he's a tiger." Kris puffed out his cheeks and his stomach. "Rest of the time, Shamu."

They laughed. Mom and Dad had taken them to SeaWorld just before Dad's accident. As Shamu, the killer whale, rose out of his pool, they had looked at each other and both said, "Uncle Kale."

Kyle felt close to Kris on top of Hildebrand Hill. It had been years since Grandpa had thrown one of his last-minute Sunday-afternoon barbecues on the front lawn. My fourth-place finish yesterday was worth a celebration, Kyle thought, and I'm happy and a little scared.

He wondered what Kris thought about it. Not really Kris's style to think too much. The Intruder keeps his eyes on what's ahead. No mirror driving.

"Look who's here." Kris elbowed him. Cowgirls were piling out of a van. "One for you, li'l bro. Do they love racers, especially after they get their pictures in the paper."

He hadn't thought the picture on the front page of

the Sunday sports section looked much like him, but he'd enjoyed the headline: "Another Hildebrand Coming on Strong." He got almost as much space as Gary, who had won the race in another thrilling duel with Ruff on their way to big-time NASCAR careers. The reporter who interviewed Kyle wanted to know all about high school, and he told her about the quintet. The reporter called Mr. G Kyle's other crew chief. It was pretty stupid.

He had thought about inviting Nicole to the barbecue. They could go on together to Mr. G's dinner. Friends and girlfriends were always welcome on Hildebrand Hill, but he wasn't sure she would be comfortable. Maybe, he thought, she would be too judgmental about his family or they would find her too New York—or maybe it's you, Kyle, not ready to handle your worlds colliding. She's got moves, she can be cool, and everybody would be nice to her because of you; even Uncle Kale could be a charmer at a party, so what's your problem? Maybe you don't want Jimmie and Nicole in the same place. Why? Maybe your problem is you think too much. Mirror driving. Keep your eyes up front.

Kris pulled him down the steps to the lawn. Low clouds of smoke drifted off the barbecues where Jackman and some of the crew were grilling burgers, franks, chicken parts, racks of ribs, and heaps of pork strips. Tables were crowded with corn, baked beans, salads, mounds of chips, soda, beer, even Jump. Once Kris reached the cowgirls, Kyle was able to slip away from him. Kris could handle a herd of cowgirls by himself.

Neighbors and friends and cousins he hadn't seen in a while were hugging and pounding shoulders. Sir Walter cruised among them, kissing, squeezing. He spotted Kyle, beckoned him over. "That was something, Kyle. That was racing with your head."

Kyle tried to sort out what he was feeling. How could you be happy and scared at the same time?

Mom and Dad were talking to Aunt Susan and a tall, gaunt man in white pants, a white shirt open to his belly button, and flip-flops. Kyle had never seen him before.

Uncle Kale was holding court in a hammock, a beer can balanced on his stomach. He looked happy.

Kyle looked for Jimmie, finally found her in a cloud of barbecue smoke flipping burgers. Her hair was pulled back and up, and her face was beet red.

"Hey."

"Hey." She looked glad to see him. "How'd the inquiry go? I left right away, back in the hauler with Billy."

"They hollered at Boyd some for show, but his car

was wrecked so they didn't do anything. You were reading my mind."

"Nah, I just figured you were smart enough to do what I would do."

"Hope you told Uncle Kale that." It felt like trash talking in the band room. Felt easy.

"Yeah, right." She looked around, lowered her voice. "It was you who made him hire me back."

"Who said that?"

"No secrets in the pits. Thanks."

"Band fags need all the help they can get."

"C'mon, gimme a break, I didn't mean to say that."

"Sure you did."

"Well, I'm sorry." She flashed her big smile. "Bunch of the crew's going to Lobo tonight—the cowgirls got asked back. Guess why. Wanna go? My treat?"

"I got something to do."

"Real music, huh?"

"I'll take a rain check." When she nodded, he plunged on, "Maybe you'll come to a concert sometime."

"I'd like that." Her million-dollar smile disappeared. "You gonna have time for everything?"

That stopped him. "Time?"

"The second car and all."

"Jimmie!" It was Jackman down the barbecue line. "You servin' or jabberin'?"

They looked up to see a line waiting for burgers. "Later," said Jimmie.

He filled a plate with barbecue and corn and wandered the lawn, enjoying the smiles and the nods, the pats and the pinches. A couple of weeks ago he had been invisible. He chatted with Gary, maybe the first time alone, he thought, certainly the first time driver to driver. Gary told him to watch out for Slater, who was sneaky where Ruff was only mean, and wished him good luck.

He was surprised to see Lloyd Rogers. First time he'd ever seen a black face on Hildebrand Hill that didn't belong to someone who worked for the family. Rogers was talking to Uncle Kale, who had actually swung his legs over the side of the hammock so he was sitting up. It looked serious. Was Uncle Kale interviewing him? Maybe they were going to hire him to drive. He felt a flash of anger. Wait a minute, Kylie, you want out, right?

Right.

There were a lot of people on the lawn who seemed to know him better than he knew them. A lot of them had seen the story in the paper, and they congratulated him.

He checked his watch. Give himself time to get over to Mr. G's house.

"Kyle, good job." It was Randall with his wife. Away from the track, in a bright-blue shirt and tan pants, he didn't look so old. "You know Melissa."

"Great race, Kyle." She was a teacher at the high school, but he had never been in her class. She turned to Randall. "Kyle plays trombone in the band."

Before he could correct her, Randall said, "Multitalented young man. Gonna be a lot on your plate when the new deal starts."

"Randall may be in that new deal," said Melissa.

"I been talking to your dad and grandpa," said Randall. "Gonna need car chiefs and crew chiefs."

"You'll quit driving?" said Kyle.

"It's time," said Melissa.

"I'll miss you bumping me," said Kyle, and they all laughed.

Dad called from across the lawn and waved him over. He was still standing with Aunt Susan and the gaunt man in white. Mom was gone.

"Kyle, this is Wolf Unger. He does TV commercials for Family Brands."

Unger didn't shake hands, but he did look Kyle up and down, twice. "Good-looking family," he said. He had a slight accent. "You're the musical one?"

"Takes after his mom," said Aunt Susan.

"With luck and good weather we should be able to

shoot this in one day," said Unger. "We want to get it on the air during the Charlotte race."

"We start painting the grandstands tomorrow," said Aunt Susan.

"Should be painting today," said Unger.

"It's Sunday," said Aunt Susan.

Unger rolled his eyes. "In my business, Sunday is Monday."

Dad said, "They're shooting at Goshen Raceway next weekend, you, me, and Kris. There's a whole script. We're arguing over who gets the car."

"And then two more cars appear," said Aunt Susan. "It is so cool."

Everybody knows what's going on except me, thought Kyle. Another flash of anger. He wondered if Kris knew. But Kris didn't really care. Just give him a girl, a beer, and a ride, he was happy.

"Don't get a haircut," said Unger. "We'll have a stylist."

Everybody tells me what to do. The anger spread.

Unger started to turn away, then said, "What is it you play?"

"What?"

"The trumpet," said Aunt Susan. "He's very good."

Kyle was surprised. Had she ever heard him?

"Marching band?" said Unger.

"Yes, and we have a brass quintet, classical and jazz."

Unger looked interested. He plucked a business card out of a pocket, handed it to Kyle. "Have someone contact me. Might be a nice touch. A grace note, if you will."

THIRTY-TWO

It was Mom's idea to bring Hildebrand Racing caps, T-shirts, and number 12 die-cast car models for Mr. G's kids. Who knew he had kids? He thought it would be too weird under the circumstances. The other members of the quintet would think he was buttering up, and Mr. G would think he was being ironical at a time when racing and music were colliding.

But Mom had insisted it was the right thing to do, and she had even gone to the race shop after church to pick out the gifts. Kyle almost left them in the Camaro when he got to Mr. G's house, an ordinary-looking ranch on a street of ordinary-looking ranches on the other side of Goshen. But then he saw the little plastic kiddie pool and a cheap metal swing set in the scrubby backyard. There were kids. Nicole's Honda and Todd's Escalade were already in the driveway. He was glad to see they hadn't come together.

Mr. G was happy to see him and delighted with the gifts for his kids. "Marie, will you look at this."

His wife, Marie, was dumpy and plain, not what Kyle would have expected, but she was also nicer than he would have expected and a terrific cook. She had made two kinds of lasagna, chicken, and a watermelon salad. They ate on the deck in the back while the two little kids played in the yard. Nice kids. Kyle was glad to see that his backup, Justin, wasn't there.

Mr. G put on the number 12 cap. "That was great what you said in the paper. The principal called me this morning." Kyle blanked for a moment. What had he said? "He loved that crew chief line. So did I, after I found out what it meant." He grinned. "You know, people, a crew chief tells the car chief and the pit crew and even the driver what to do. So a little more respect, please."

They all started asking questions at once, even Nicole. Why was the car faster this week, did he have a plan from the beginning of the race, why was Boyd so pissed off? What was going to happen when Kris came back?

He enjoyed the attention, answered carefully without

saying too much, especially about Kris and the second car. Boyd was pissed off, he explained, because after finally getting a sponsor, he had wrecked his car.

"Boyd's spotter should have seen he was heading into the Dodge," said Del.

"I guess he didn't have a sexy voice in his ear," said Nicole.

"Saw that film," said Jesse. *"Two Girls and a Guy,* Robert Downey Jr. and Heather Graham."

"You made that up," snapped Nicole. She seemed annoyed.

"You got another race coming up?" asked Todd.

There was a moment of silence, then Mr. G said, "Let's burn that bridge when we come to it. Marie made a chocolate cake."

They started chattering about the Brooklyn Brass audition a little more than two weeks away and lost track of time. Mr. G eventually shooed them out, reminding them it was a school night. At the door, Kyle remembered the director's card and gave it to Mr. G.

"He said maybe we could do something in the commercial he's shooting."

Mr. G held the card as if it were a lottery ticket.

"Want to stop by?" said Nicole.

"Why not?"

"Curb your enthusiasm."

"Yeah, I want to. That better?"

He followed her home. The house was dark. They sat outside on the glider, so close he couldn't see her face in the dim porch light without turning. Their lips brushed.

She pulled back a little. "That number you ran on Mr. G was pretty slick."

"Number?" It took him a moment. "That was real. It was the director's idea, not mine."

"Oh." She sounded pleased. "I thought you did it to buy more time for racing."

"I don't know what I'm doing." That hadn't quite come out right, but he didn't have a chance to play it over.

"You're telling me," she said, and kissed him.

They had their hands inside each other's shirts when headlights appeared at the top of the driveway.

"Shit," said Nicole.

Her parents seemed cool, a bearded dad in cargo pants and a mom in a flowered skirt. They said they had snuck out of a faculty concert. They invited him in, but Nicole reminded them it was a school night.

He had the dream that night, racing three wide, only this time he was caught between Jimmie and Nicole. He wasn't sure it was really a dream, more like imagination in that floating time before you go over the edge into sleep. In any case, he didn't make himself wake up. He wanted to see how it turned out. But it just ended, going nowhere.

THIRTY-THREE

He woke up thinking it was going to be a sweet, easy week. Nobody would be on his case. It started that way. By the time he came downstairs Monday morning, Dad had left for the race shop. Besides 12A they were building a show car for Family Brands to display. There would be no performance engine in it, but it had to look exactly like the real race cars.

Mom was sleeping late. He remembered that had happened before, when Dad went back to racing after his accident. She hadn't wanted him to go back. There had been arguments. But Sir Walter had retired and said that the fans wanted a Hildebrand in the Hildebrand car. Grandma Karen and Aunt Susan were in the house every day getting Kris and Kyle off to school while Mom slept. It lasted only a month or so. One day she started playing the piano again, and soon after that she was waking up in time for them all to have breakfast together. After Dad stopped racing, she started giving lessons. She loved doing it. She seemed much happier, even happier than before his accident. It was only later that Kyle figured out they needed the money.

And now she was sleeping late again. He wondered if she was avoiding the world because Kris got hurt or because he was racing. Or both.

Kyle tried not to think about that, enjoying the quiet time in the kitchen. He had a turkey-and-cheese sandwich for breakfast as he checked the ball scores on ESPN and glanced through the sports pages. There was a story about the return of Hildebrand Racing that quoted Family Brands vice president David Winik saying that "Hildebrand is a Family Brand, a perfect fit for our customers."

Toward the end of the story Uncle Kale was quoted as refusing to say who would be the driver of number 12A, the "clone of the Blue Shadow." The reporter speculated that drivers being considered included Boyd Jurgensen and Lloyd Rogers. No wonder Rogers had been at the party.

Kyle felt a pinprick of anger. How come I wasn't

mentioned? Not that I would take the ride. Would I? Or do I just want the chance to say no?

He felt better at school, a celebrity, waves and nods and fist bumps in the hallways, even from seniors, smiles from girls who had always looked through him. Teachers congratulated him. No hassle on his homework, or lack of.

He showed up late for quintet because the football coach cornered him in the hallway and demanded to hear about the fight in the garage. But his chair was empty and waiting for him. Justin, sitting alone in the back with his trumpet on his lap, pumped his fist as Kyle walked in. Jesse blew a tuba squawk.

Nicole squeezed his arm as he sat down next to her. Like they were a couple. He wondered again what would have happened if her parents had stayed at the concert.

He thought he played poorly, but no one commented. When they finished the rehearsal, Mr. G invited Justin up and handed out music for the three-trumpet flourish that opened the triumphal march in *Aida*. They had never played any opera before.

"Wolf and I were thinking," said Mr. G, "it might work in the commercial."

"You talked to the guy already?" said Kyle.

"Texted him last night, talked first thing this morning. He told me to prepare a few pieces to knock his socks off, although I must say he sounded like one of those Hollywood types who don't wear socks."

Kyle remembered the flip-flops.

Out in the parking lot Nicole said, "Sorry about last night."

"I'll take a rain check," he said. Got two rain checks now, he thought.

She hooked an arm around his waist. First Public Show of Affection, he thought, proud and embarrassed. He glanced around. No one was paying attention.

"Next weekend?" she said. "My parents have a conference in Atlanta. And you don't have a race."

"The commercial." When he felt her arm start to slide away, he said, "Come with me?"

"Sure."

He looped his arm around her shoulders.

It was almost suppertime when he got to the race shop, but there was no sense that the workday was winding down. Kris, Jackman, and Billy were working on number 12 in a repair bay, and Dad, Randall, Jimmie, and the mechanics and fabricators were working on 12A and the show car on the main floor. The skeletons of backup cars were lined up like museum dinosaurs. Uncle Kale bustled back and forth among the cars, pointing and snapping orders.

He felt out of place, sorry he had come. Why had he come? He hadn't even thought it through when he'd left Nicole in the parking lot.

"Kyle!" Uncle Kale was waving him over. "In the car."

Gratefully he climbed in 12A and worked his butt and back into the seat. "Needs more padding."

"That's what you're here for," said Randall.

"Meet twelve A's car chief," said Uncle Kale.

"Your car chief," said Randall, patting Kyle's shoulder.

Uncle Kale looked away.

Kyle climbed out without saying anything. He felt like he was in the middle of an *X-Files* rerun. *My* car chief? What about Lloyd Rogers?

It was going to be a long week after all.

THIRTY-FOUR

Fresh coats of white and deep-blue paint glistened in
the Saturday-morning sun. Even from the hill overlooking the track, Kyle could smell the paint. He imagined
the grandstand still sticky, but Goshen Raceway looked
sparkling and new, the way he remembered it from
childhood, when the family was riding high.

"It's beautiful," said Nicole. "A jewel box."

He liked her response, felt proud. Below them several
hundred local people were being ushered into the
Walter Hildebrand section of the grandstand by production assistants. One newspaper notice, a couple of
radio spots, and an e-mail invitation to the Hildebrand
fan club had brought them out to be in the commercial,
in return for lunch and a T-shirt. The paint better be dry

on those seats, he thought.

On the newly shiny black track, Wolf, the director, was supervising the placement of the cars. A camera crew was setting up in the bed of a truck. Kyle spotted Jackman and the crew stuffing themselves at a long food table while Dad, Sir Walter, and Uncle Kale stood talking with Family Brands types, down to their shirtsleeves in the heat. Dad was wearing the new Family Brands fire suit. When had he been fitted for that?

Nicole said, "Shouldn't you be down there?"

"Kris isn't here yet."

She laughed. "Sibling rivalry. You're not going to stand around waiting for him, right?"

He wondered if he felt annoyed because she saw through him or because it made him feel childish. Why do I think so much? Why do I have to be such a mirror driver?

"Let's go." He grabbed her hand. They slung their gig bags over their shoulders and danced down the hill to the track.

"Oh, my God, look!" she said. He followed her pointing finger to a far section of the grandstand, where fresh deep-blue letters spelled out:

KYLE HILDEBRAND

"That's new," he said. "For the commercial."

"Didn't you use to race here?"

"When I was a kid." When she made a funny face, he said, "I started when I was five, in quarter-midgets and go-karts. By the time I was into modifieds, the action moved to Monroe Speedway."

"That was after your grandfather retired and your dad got hurt." She smiled at his surprise. "Don't you think I Googled you? Even my dad was impressed. This is the big Hildebrand comeback."

"We'll see." He felt uncomfortable. It was one thing to read about it in the paper, another to actually talk about it.

She squeezed his hand. He wondered if she really got it. If he did.

Jimmie was the first to spot them. She marched across the track toward them, square shouldered, her red braid swinging, and gave Nicole an obvious once-over before she extended a hand. "Hi, I'm Jimmie. I'm with the crew."

"I'm Nicole. I'm with the band."

That broke the ice a little, Kyle thought. At least Jimmie grinned. He couldn't see Nicole's face past the cloud of curly black hair.

"You better get dressed for the shoot, Kyle. Your suit's in the makeup trailer." Jimmie pointed to a construction trailer in the garage area. "The band's in a tent behind the trailer."

"See you later." Nicole kissed him before she headed for the tent.

Jimmie watched her go. "You guys making music?"

He decided to ignore that. "Where's Kris?"

"This some kind of race to see who arrives last? He's on his way."

He followed her inside the double-wide. Two identical fire suits hung from a clothes pole, and a woman was sitting in a barber chair dabbing at a thick layer of makeup on her face. Her lipstick was bright red. She spotted him in the mirror and jumped up. "You must be Kris."

"Kyle," he said.

"He's gonna be better than Kris," said Jimmie.

"Better at what?" The woman cackled and stuck out her hand. "Hi, Kyle, I'm Darlene, gonna make you up."

He felt embarrassed by the bold way Darlene was looking at him. She was younger than he had first thought.

"Better driver," said Jimmie. On her way to the door, she said, "They're getting impatient out there. It's hot."

Darlene said, "Get dressed, Kyle. Then I'll do your face."

"Right here?"

"You've got something I haven't seen before?"

He stripped down to his underwear and pulled on the suit. He couldn't tell if it was the one he had worn in the races or a new one. When he sat in the barber chair, Darlene covered the suit with a smock. "Just a little powder to cut down the shine," said Darlene. He had never been made up before. Once he relaxed, he liked the feel of the soft brush. He closed his eyes as she dabbed at his lids.

"The redhead your girlfriend?"

"She works on the cars."

"She'd like to work on you, Kyle, trust me." Darlene trimmed his hair around his ears and rubbed in gel. She combed it up. Looked like Kris's hair. "There you go. I'll be outside, touch you up when you need it."

He climbed down from the trailer in time to see Kris roar onto the track on one of Jackman's Harleys. A cowgirl was hanging on to him. He circled the track once, spotted Kyle, and made a gravel-spitting stop a few feet away.

"Hey," said Kris. He was laughing. He looked wasted and happy. Back to normal. "You must be Kyle. Heard a lot about you. They say you can drive."

THIRTY-FIVE

Shooting the commercial was almost as boring as sitting through environmental science at Goshen High. The director stomped around like a skinny Uncle Kale, shouting orders, complaining about the bright sunlight, pushing cameras around. Then he'd go off to check the picture setups on a bank of TV monitors in an air-conditioned trailer while almost everyone else baked in the heat.

Kyle spent most of the time in the makeup trailer with Kris, Dad, and an assistant director, going over their scene. The lines were simple. The three of them argued over which one of them got to drive number 12 until Sir Walter appeared and said, "Easy, boys. Here at Family Brands there's something for everyone." The camera then zoomed out to reveal two more identical cars. In the next scene they would be driving three wide down the track while Sir Walter waved a flag with the Family Brands logo.

Kyle remembered his dream. But in the script Dad was in the middle car.

"Pretty stupid," said Kris cheerfully.

"Let's just get through this," said Dad. He was nervous.

"We'll race the cars," said Kris.

"You are joking," said the assistant director, a young woman, looking horrified.

"Then forget it," said Kris, pretending to start tearing his script.

"He's joking," said Dad, glaring at Kris.

"I'll take the show car and still whip Kyle's ass," said Kris. Something in his voice flipped a switch in back of Kyle's mind. He thought of Grandpa's porch. Kris is not joking.

"Save it for Charlotte," said Kyle.

"You won't be there," said Kris. "You're retired."

He really wants to race me, to beat me, thought Kyle. Where does that come from? It excited him. Pleased him.

The makeup woman started touching them up again. "They're ready for you."

Kris was totally relaxed in front of the camera. Dad seemed as self-conscious as Kyle felt. Each of them had to yell, "No, I'm the designated driver." Kris was the only one who didn't sound as if he were reading lines. He meant it. The crowd broke out laughing and applauded him. On the sixth take, when he yelled "How many times do I have to tell you, I'm the designated driver!" even the director applauded and yelled, "Cut! That's it. Let's break."

The assistant director led Kyle to a spot in front of the grandstand crowd, where Mr. G and the brass players were sweating in their marching band uniforms. They managed the trumpet flourish from *Aida* in three takes, then played a few minutes of Dixieland before they went to lunch at the long tables.

Kyle was too hot to eat more than a turkey sandwich and drink three bottles of water. Nicole just drank water.

"What if you have to pee during a race?" she said.

"Most of it comes out in sweat," said Kyle, but when he noticed Del laughing, he added, "The rest just comes out. Dries fast."

Mr. G wrinkled his face. "Sounds horrible."

"Unless you're leading," said Kyle.

•••

In the final big scene, Kyle, Kris, and Dad were supposed to sprint to their cars, climb in, and drive off while the people in the grandstand clapped and cheered. They did it eight times, which took most of the rest of the afternoon, since after they were in the cars, the director had to stop the action while crews ran out to help them put on their helmets and hook up the head and neck restraints. Kris tried his old jackknife into the car, and even after he made it on the second try, the director told him they all had to climb in the usual way and at about the same speed. He sulked about that but agreed. Then he shot ahead of the other two cars, and they had to restart. Everybody was cranky by the time it worked and the three cars, door to door, were moving slowly past the grandstand as Sir Walter waved the flag.

They were halfway around the track, Kris on the outside near the wall, when the public address system crackled and the director shouted, "Cut. That's a wrap for the day. Thank you, everybody." Everybody cheered.

Dad dropped back in the show car and turned into the pits.

Kris stuck his hand out his window and waved Kyle alongside. "Let's see what you got." He mashed the gas.

Without thinking, Kyle accelerated after him.

They were back on grandpa's porch and it was exhilarating. Somewhere in the distance he could hear Dad and Uncle Kale yelling, but they had yelled on Hildebrand Hill when he and Kris were racing trikes, so what was the difference now when the porch was a quarter-mile oval and the chairs and relatives they slalomed around were production assistants and video equipment?

Just racing.

Number 12A felt a little loose in the turns. Have to tell Uncle Kale about it. Car feels like a lot to handle but eager to go and hair-trigger on the gas. For the first two laps he was right behind Kris, and by the third he was back alongside. Kris grinned at him and cocked a finger and shot ahead half a length, but Kyle caught him a lap later. The cars were a match. It was about who was a better driver.

Dad and Uncle Kale were running along the yellow line, frantically waving them in, and Sir Walter's deep voice was booming over the PA, "That's it, boys, bring 'em in, bring 'em in right now," but there was no way they were going to stop right now—they were going to keep going around the porch until one of them drove the other off into Grandma Karen's flower bed even if the flowers were made of concrete. Let's see what you got, big bro, this time I'm gonna whip your ass without a rake. I kept your seat warm, and now I own it.

Kyle took the lead on the sixth lap and blocked when Kris tried to pass.

Kris tapped him.

If he hadn't expected it, he would have spun into the wall.

The thought was an electric shock: Kris was going to do it again, he was going to bump him out of the way even if it meant wrecking him to win this silly little jerk-off race in front of people who weren't going to appreciate what he did because their jobs depended on these two cars making it to the races. Kris was going to do it because he had to win.

That's all he has.

That's not my problem.

I don't have to let him win. I just might have the car and the smarts to beat him today, to use his craziness against him, to lure him up into a corner and leave him smoking, let him wreck himself.

Am I crazy too?

The family is depending on us.

Kyle blocked right, and when Kris tried to pass him on the inside, he let him go. Kyle flipped him the bird as he passed, just to let him know I gave you this one, big bro, you didn't win it.

Kyle cut left and dove into the pits. Sir Walter was waiting for him, the flag tucked under his arm, smiling, his thumbs up.

THIRTY-SIX

By the time he got to Nicole's house, it was night. He saw the burning red tip of a cigarette before he made out the cloud of black hair and then Nicole on the porch glider.

"You don't smoke."

"Today I do." She was in a mood.

"That's stupid. Paying to get lung cancer."

"You should talk." She sounded cranky. "How can you blow a trumpet after hours of breathing all that smoke and fumes and crap at the track?"

He plucked the cigarette out of her hand and ground it out on the porch deck. He expected her to react, but she didn't. "You okay?"

"I thought you were coming hours ago."

"Sorry. I got your voice mail but I didn't have time to call back." He reached for her. She pulled away once, then let him hold her hands. "When did you guys split?"

"Your dad and this really fat guy—"

"My uncle Kale."

"Whoops." She laughed. "Well, they were screaming and the commercial people started herding everybody out, and Mr. G thought we should go too."

"You got any beer?"

"Let's see some ID." She stood up and hugged him. "I thought you weren't going to come. That you had something better to do."

"It was sort of intense." He liked the way she led him into the house, pushed him into a chair at the kitchen table, and plunked a cold can in front of him.

"You guys must have caught hell."

"Well. There was some discussion." He waited for the day to fall into place in his head, like a shuffled deck. "They screamed for a while, but then the director said the race was great, they got it on tape, and we had to watch it and then redo parts of it. They might use it in the next commercial. They're gonna write some lines about how even in the best of families we try to be the best and to best each other."

"Here at Family Brands"—she did a pretty good imitation of Sir Walter—"we try to kill each other."

Kyle laughed. He felt close to her. He was glad she had seen it. "Kris got props for being aggressive and I got props for being cautious. Win-win."

"At least it's over."

"Really. Coulda been ugly."

"No, I mean it's over for you. Kris is back and you're free."

"Free?" He knew what she meant but he stalled.

"To play with the quintet. To do what you want." She stared at him across the table. "That is what you want."

"Yeah." It didn't sound positive to him.

Her eyes narrowed. "You want to keep racing?"

He still felt close enough to take a chance. "I'm not sure." But he wasn't sure if he wasn't sure. I'm a work in progress. He wasn't sure about anything, even if he really wanted to be here right now.

"You drove off the track."

"Kris was out of control. We could have wrecked both cars. After everything everybody's been working for."

"Sounds like you're back where we started." She sounded sad, not angry. "I think you really want to race."

"I said I'm not sure." It sounded harsh when it came. She winced. Maybe I'm being too hard on Nicole. Maybe she thinks we'll never get together if I race.

Sounds like a soap opera. "Sorry. I guess I'm confused."

She came around the table then and sat on his lap. They were kissing when he felt a buzzing at his groin. It was a moment before he realized it was his phone vibrating.

"Yeah?"

"Team meeting tomorrow morning at eleven, the shop." It was Jimmie. Nicole slid off his lap and went back to her chair.

"What for?" said Kyle.

"Ask Sir Walter—he called it."

He turned off the phone and put it on the table. "Team meeting tomorrow morning."

She popped open another beer. "Mr. G called a rehearsal for tomorrow. At noon."

"Sunday?"

"The audition is coming up in ten days."

"You think we won't get it after being in a national commercial?"

"That sounds pretty arrogant." She took a long pull on the can. "Even for a trumpet player."

"What about for a race driver?" This time he was trying to be harsh. Some part of him wanted to be out of here.

"That's what you really want to be, isn't it?" Now she sounded harsh.

218

"At the track you seemed to get it. I thought you understood where I was at."

"Maybe not. Where are you . . . at?" Now she was mimicking him.

"I just don't want anybody boxing me in, telling me what to do."

"You just don't want to make a commitment." She cracked open another can.

"Commitment, no, not if it means I can't keep my options open."

"Keep my options open." She was slurring words. "A girl with the crew and a girl with the band. Lucky boy's got a pit lizard and a horn ho." Her face seemed to be disappearing into her curly black hair.

He tried to think of something to say, but in the silence she kicked back her chair. "I'm going up. You can come if you want."

He waited until he heard her footsteps on the stairs before he left the house.

THIRTY-SEVEN

When he got to the race shop at eleven on the nose, Sir Walter's office was already packed. The way people looked up and nodded, he knew they had been waiting for him. They cleared space for him to come into the room, but he shook his head and stayed by the door. Kris was on the couch between Jackman and Randall, smiley and mellow, his eyes barely open. At least somebody got some last night.

"We all here?" said Dad. He was perched on a corner of Sir Walter's huge desk. Uncle Kale was leaning against the opposite corner. Sir Walter sat back in his throne, scanning the group. Spotting, Kyle thought. He felt those cold deep-blue eyes flick over him.

Kyle looked for Jimmie. She was squatting in a corner,

alongside Billy, who was in a wooden chair. Most of the crew members and mechanics were squatting.

"Okay, here's the deal," said Dad. "Family Brands sold truckloads of Jump and Yum Cakes in the tristate area last week, and they figure it was Hildebrand fans who bought them. So they're starting their big ad campaign next week around the Charlotte race. They expect two competitive cars in that race, and they're thinking about a third by the end of the season. Can we deliver?"

Jackman and the crew stomped and yelled as if they were at a football pep rally. Dad grinned and looked at Sir Walter, who smiled and nodded. Uncle Kale's face didn't change expression. When the noise died down, Uncle Kale said, "Here's how it's going to happen. Shop opens at six A.M., closes when we're done. Every day. Don't matter if you're in the seat or in the rear with the gear, everybody's expected to do his"—he paused to blink at Jimmie—"or her job. Any questions?"

"Yo." Kris waved from the couch. "Who's driving the second car?"

Kyle was surprised to see Uncle Kale and Dad both turn to Sir Walter, who leaned forward across his desk. "Not decided yet. No secret, we've been talking to Lloyd Rogers. Among others. Family Brands would prefer a Hildebrand in the seat, and they don't mean me." He chuckled and a few people laughed along, but his eyes stayed cold, and Kyle felt a chill run up his back.

He slipped out the door. He imagined all the eyes in the room burning into his back. Hot and cold.

Mom was sipping coffee on the deck when he got home. She was in her robe. He grabbed a soda and went out on the deck.

"Just back from church?" She sounded sarcastic.

"Team meeting."

"I know. Big decisions."

He sat down alongside her and gazed up Hildebrand Hill at Grandpa's wraparound porch.

"Mr. Sievers called. He wants to know if he should keep the Saturday hour open for you."

"What do you think I should do?"

She took his hand and squeezed it. "I think you should find out if there's room for a trumpet in a race car."

"Keep your options open."

"I'm glad it's not my decision," she said. "How can you choose between your husband and your son?"

They sat quietly until Dad came home. Dad kissed her on top of her head. She raised her other hand to hold his.

Dad said, "Sir Walter wants to see you, Kyle. He'll be back up the hill in about an hour."

THIRTY-EIGHT

He drove into the Goshen High parking lot without a plan. Mr. G had called the rehearsal for noon. There was still time to show up and claim his chair. But he wasn't sure that was what he wanted to do. He felt as though he was looking for a sign, a waving green flag telling him to go, a red flag to stop. A black flag signaling him out of the race.

He was going to have to make his choices all by himself. The only flag for a work in progress was the yellow flag: Keep moving ahead with caution.

He drove around to the back of the school into a staff lot that band members were allowed to use on weekends. It was outside the door closest to the music rooms. He spotted Mr. G's Chevy Suburban, Todd's

Escalade, Jesse's Jeep, a Toyota he didn't recognize, and a delivery van from Del's family's restaurant. He didn't see Nicole's Honda. Either she wasn't there or she had come with someone else. She could use a ride this morning, the way she'd been drinking last night. Jesse probably picked her up. Todd would be too weird. But I'm not sure of anything.

He circled the lot, half hoping someone would come out and wave him in, or Nicole would drive in and he'd have no choice except to park. Half hoping. He wondered, If I never saw these people again, would I miss them? Nicole's honk and the smart-ass talk about Mr. G and movies? Would I miss playing with them? Would I miss the trumpet? That feeling of safety in the music? Is it all the same choice?

I don't have to make that choice, remember? Keep your options open.

He remembered Nicole in the parking lot asking him, "You going to be able to handle it all?"

I still don't know. But I want to try.

He drove out of the lot and back onto the main road toward Goshen.

Jimmie's black Mustang was parked outside the race shop. Jackman's Harley was nearby, along with Dad's pickup, Uncle Kale's Explorer, and Billy's ancient Corvette. He wondered where Kris was. He wouldn't mind talking to Jimmie, but not in a crowd. He remembered her saying, "I'm sure you'll do the right thing."

I hope I figure out what the right thing is.

He drove on aimlessly, almost reaching the foothills of the Buckline Mountains before he turned back. After a while he found himself circling Goshen Raceway. He passed the airport behind the parking lots. A small plane was taking off. Probably a student pilot, he thought. Dad had worked out a deal with a flying school. There had been big plans for the airport once, but they were based on Goshen Raceway becoming a stop in one of the NASCAR regional series. Another casualty of Dad's accident. Monroe Speedway had gotten the races. But Goshen Raceway could make a comeback with the Hildebrand family. Grandpa had been talking about extending the runway for small jets. Once Hildebrand Racing was running two cars, three cars, at least one of them on a major NASCAR circuit, we'd need a jet runway for drivers who wanted to test at Goshen or maybe even race here if we made the track bigger.

We?

He circled the raceway on the access road that ran around it. He parked outside the chain link fence, on the little hill near the rear gate, his favorite spot. He remembered tearing around the little go-kart track that had been here, his first racing track, little more than a circular dirt path ringed with rubber tires. Racing was fun then.

When had it started being fun again?

That thought surprised him. It *had* become fun again. The answer didn't surprise him.

After Kris got hurt.

He felt guilty, then remembered how Mom had gotten back to the piano after Dad's accident. He wondered if she felt guilty about that. Someday he would find a way to talk to her about it. I can talk to Mom.

He heard a truck motor growling and looked down at the track. A pickup filled with camera equipment was pulling out of the garage area toward the main entrance. He remembered that the assistant director was coming back today for shots of the show car circling the track. Distant shots, no close-ups, so a member of the crew would drive the car.

A Family Brands number 12 Ford pulled out of the garage area and drove slowly around the track. He could tell from the sound of the engine that it was the show car. From the way the driver drove deep into the corner and let the car drift up the track on the straightaway, Kyle imagined him learning the track, finding the line, studying for a future race. One of the crew had driver dreams.

Did he?

The car passed the grandstand. He was surprised to see his name still up there. Did you think it was just for the commercial?

A noise overhead drowned out the show car's street engine. Kyle looked up to watch the student pilot circle the airport before coming down for a bumpy landing. By the time the plane was on the ground, the show car was gone and the sky and the track were silent.

He was alone.

Without thinking about it, he pulled his gig bag out of the trunk and took out the trumpet. He walked to the top of the hill where the go-kart track had been. He blew a few long notes before he found himself playing "Autumn Leaves."

He imagined Mom's Oscar Peterson piano version spilling a waterfall of notes down the hill and through the chain link fence, rippling over the freshly painted grandstand seats and onto the black ribbon of track while his Dizzy Gillespie trumpet version found the line and held it, lap after lap, until the checkered flag came down.

He closed his eyes, and the raceway and the bright spring afternoon disappeared. He was lost in the music.

When he was exhausted, when his breath was gone and his lips throbbed, he stopped. He felt chilled.

"That was beautiful." Jimmie's green eyes looked damp. The show car was parked behind her.

"That was you on the track." When she nodded, he said, "Gonna race?"

"Thinking about it. You?"

"Thinking about it." He suddenly realized how that must sound to her. He had choices. She was the one with driver dreams.

"That's okay." Had she read his mind again? She pointed at the trumpet dangling from his hand. "I had no idea how good you were. I thought you just—" She stopped.

"What?"

"I thought it was something you did because Kris didn't."

"It started that way, I guess."

"And now they're going to make you choose." She came close enough to touch the trumpet, run a finger along the tube until it flared out into the bell. "I talked to your girlfriend yesterday. She really wants you to concentrate on music."

"Everybody's got their own idea what I should do with my life."

"What are you going to do?"

"I'm going to do it all."

Then they were kissing. He felt the heat rising

through his body, chasing the chill, reviving him. She smelled of sweat and gas.

She pushed him away. "Not here, not now." She put her hand on his face. "A trumpet player can always get a girl," she said, "but even a great driver needs a spotter."

THIRTY-NINE

Sir Walter was waiting for him on the porch, sitting in a white wicker armchair. He was holding a picture of himself and Grandma Karen in Victory Lane after he won his first Cup race, forty years ago.

"Miss her every day," he said. "She was the one kept Hildebrand together after I was finished and your dad was hurt."

Here it comes, Kyle thought. Sir Walter is going to order me into the car the way Great-grandpa Fred ordered him in and he ordered Dad and Dad didn't have to order Kris. . . . That sounded like the begats in the Bible.

"Wanted to tell you, meant a lot what you did these past couple weeks. You were the one kept Hildebrand together. Gave us time to make the deal that's gonna put us back in the show. I'm hoping you'll stay with it, starting in Charlotte next week."

"What if I don't want to drive?" It burst out and left a sour taste in his mouth.

Sir Walter didn't blink. "Don't want you to act against your nature. Never work."

"Didn't work with Uncle Ken."

Sir Walter blinked this time. "I made a mistake with Kenny. Drove him so hard, I drove him away. I think about that a lot. You look surprised."

He was. Hard to think of Sir Walter as a mirror driver. Keep your eyes on the road ahead. Sir Walter put the picture down on a table and pushed himself up out of the chair.

"Might've made a mistake with your dad, I was so set on somebody following me. Kris was a natural. From day one you could see he was born to race. No fear. He could feel the air change around a car when someone was coming up on him. All he wanted to do was get to the front and stay there." Sir Walter put a hand on Kyle's shoulder and steered him forward. "Let's walk a lap. My legs stiffen up when I just stand."

Shoulders bumping gently, they began to circle the porch. Kyle could see his house tucked into the foot of Hildebrand Hill. Were Mom and Dad looking up at the porch, wondering what Sir Walter was saying to him? Or did they know?

"When you drove off the track yesterday, when you didn't let Kris get your goat, that was something. Your uncle Kale said to me, 'You woulda done that, Daddy.' You know he calls you the Baby Blue Shadow."

"Uncle Kale?" He didn't believe it, then felt guilty. Sir Walter couldn't be playing me, could he? Got more words out of him in the last few minutes than in my whole life. Maybe he thought I was never worth talking to before.

"Always liked Blue Shadow better than Sir Walter, which sounds kind of nose in the air, but it's what the fans like that counts."

He couldn't get it out of his head. "Uncle Kale called me the Baby Blue Shadow?"

"Never say it to your face, 'fraid it might swell your head." Sir Walter chuckled. "That boy took the lawn mower motor apart when he was two. Couldn't get it back together till he was three." He laughed out loud, eyes shining. "They was some pair, Kale and Kenny. I thought they was headed right to the top. Maybe I could've got Kenny back, but I had a stiff neck those days. And I had Kerry, who was almost as good. I think Kerry might've won the cup that year he got hurt. Kale's been looking for a racer ever since."

"Now he's got Kris." The Buckline Mountains heaved up and disappeared. Lake Goshen shimmered.

"Looks that way, don't it? Kris drives like Dale Sr., like Tony Stewart. Straight ahead, get out of my way. You drive like I did. Patient, think laps ahead, never wreck a man just to win."

Dale and Tony won a lot more races than you did, thought Kyle.

"You don't need to have the mean streak, the killer instinct, to be a winner," said Sir Walter. "Of course it depends on what you call a winner."

They were back at the front door. He could see his house. Sir Walter stopped. One lap on the porch. What was he really saying to me? "Winner does his duty, treats people right, lives a life he's proud of. Winner is tough. Your dad's a winner. Very few drivers come back after getting hurt bad as your daddy did."

Cagey old fox setting me up, the Blue Shadow creeping up on me, then slinging past. He wants me to drive. For my dad. For the family. For the Brand.

And I want to drive. But my way.

"I'm not giving up music."

"Up to you. I won't let Kale or anybody pressure you to stop." Sir Walter squeezed Kyle's shoulder. "You're tough, boy. That's good."

"I'd like to see Uncle Ken."

He couldn't believe that Sir Walter's eyes were watery. "So would I."

"Bet he'd come to watch his nephews race."

"You think so?"

"If you invited him."

Sir Walter took out a handkerchief and blew his nose, an excuse to wipe his eyes. "Sounds like we got a deal, Kyle."

"Deal, Grandpa," said Kyle, trying not to cry. He stuck out his hand to shake.

Sir Walter hugged him. Kyle felt his pens digging through his shirt.

After a while Sir Walter held him out at arm's length. "Remember, Kyle, you got to establish your territory and hold it."

"I'll remember, Grandpa," he said.

"And always have a spare Sharpie so no fan walks away disappointed because they didn't get an auto-graph."

A sneak peek at Robert Lipsyte's

RAIDERS NIGHT

ONE

The Back Pack hit the gym in the early afternoon, Matt in the lead, before the yuppies marched in from work, while the young moms were rushing out to pick up their kids from day camp. Matt liked the way their hot eyes roamed over him, wondered if they knew he was still in high school, wondered if they cared. He felt big and hard. Excited. Was it the moms or what was waiting for him upstairs, the iron weights that would make him even bigger, harder. And the juice.

Brody poked him from behind with the football he always carried. "Check the headlights on the one in blue."

"Someday I'm gonna stick that ball up your ass."

"Ooooh, don't tease me, big boy."

Matt led them through the downstairs crowd of designer spandex and pastel sweats, cuties perched on shiny machines jiggling away to love songs as they pretended to work out. What did they know about working out? He liked the sense of leaving their soft world behind as he led the Back Pack up the metal steps into the stink and clang of the second floor, the real workout room.

He was glad they had beaten the linemen to the gym today. Give us a chance to get our session going without Ramp's crap.

The ironheads were there; they were always there, older white guys screaming each other into one more pec-busting rep. They wore tank tops and bandannas that looked like they were soaked in diesel fuel. One of them called out a singsong, half-mocking "Rai-derz."

Tyrell raised two fists. "Raiders rule, niggaz!"

The ironheads liked that and banged metal plates. Some of them had gone to Nearmont High and played ball.

"Matt?" The gym owner, Monty, came out of his office and beckoned him over. "New shipment's in."

Matt nodded and felt the excitement rise. Perfect timing. Load up just before camp so the juice kicks in during the two-a-days when we really need it. He flashed the Back Pack a thumbs-up. Hope they all brought their wallets.

They dressed quickly. They were jittery, psyched for the last heavy workout before camp. Tyrell, as usual, complained about the music on the upstairs speakers, a pounding mix of disco and heavy metal. The ironheads controlled those CDs. For now. See what happens if we win Conference this year.

Matt caught Pete sneaking peeks at himself in the mirror. Pete was more self-conscious than the rest of them about the pimples on his shoulders. Backne they called it. From the steroids. Price you pay. Pete's girlfriend, Lisa, wasn't so sure it was worth the price. She'd said as much, and Pete listened to her. Girls hear about the side effects, but how could they know the feeling of watching a muscle grow bigger and harder? Pete flexed his biceps when he thought no one was looking, as if to remind himself that Lisa didn't know everything.

Matt said, "Quads and glutes win games." He wondered if he was taking this captain thing too seriously.

"Tyrell says bicep curls win hot girls," said Tyrell. He mimicked Pete's flex.

Pete, embarrassed, snapped his shirt at Tyrell, who laughed and danced just out of range. They loved to watch Tyrell move. He had radar. He glided like a phantom. He was the best running back in the conference. If we stay healthy and tight, Matt thought, this could be our season. Maybe State. Senior year, what a way to go.

Out on the mats, stretching, Matt could tell Brody's mind was heading to the same place.

"We got a shot." Brody's big freckly face had that dreamy look. Probably imagining himself winning the state title. With a quarterback sneak. Not a forty-yard bomb to me or a handoff to Tyrell, but a heroic scramble out of a collapsing pocket and a desperate lunge over the goal line. Behind his back, some of the guys called him All-Brody. Dad thought he didn't throw to Matt enough. But Brody was all right. Best friend on the team.

"One day at a time," said Matt.

"You're, like, channeling Coach Mac," said Brody.

"You ready to put the bar where your mouth is?" Matt held up the clipboard with their workout schedule.

"See what I mean?"

They started with squats, lunges, and power cleans to build up their legs and lower backs for the explosive starts off the line of scrimmage. These were the most intense exercises in the daily program the coaches had laid out in the spring. Matt had come to realize that if they left those exercises to the end of the session, they would slack off, especially Pete and Brody. They preferred to work harder on the lat pull downs, the curls and flys to build up their upper bodies for the beach. But they listened to Matt. He was their leader. Tyrell had named them the Back Pack, the four starting backfield seniors. Brody, Pete, and Matt had played together since PeeWee. Tyrell had joined them as a sophomore after he came out from New York, staying at his aunt's house during the week so he could go to Nearmont High.

The linemen stomped in, Ramp bellowing, "Yo, Rydek,

4

your girls done yet?"

Before Matt could respond, Tyrell shouted, "Where you been? Stop off for lunch at the hog farm?"

Ramp cursed, raised a finger, and led the linemen into the locker room.

Matt waited until they were out of earshot. "Chill."

"Nobody cool says chill no more."

"Our last season, last chance to win Conference." He glared at Tyrell until he nodded and started pulling dumbbells off the rack. "Let's be a team."

"You always right, Cap'n Matt, sir."

Matt and Brody moved to the benches. It took a few reps to clear his head, but once Matt felt the blood pumping again, all the good feelings came back. He concentrated on visualizing his muscles swell and harden as he lay on the bench and pushed the bar up toward Brody's face. Familiar, comforting pains flooded his chest and shoulders as he fought his arms straight under 275 pounds.

"Up, c'mon, up, you pussy," growled Brody, spotting him. "You can do it."

Matt yelled as his elbows locked. Personal best.

"Good job," shouted Brody. "It's all you, man."

"Nice start," snickered Ramp, his big potato head looming above Matt. "Now put some weight on the bar." He swaggered off. The linemen would be lifting at least fifty pounds more.

5

They worked out for two hours, tapering on the rowing machines, cooling down on the treadmill. They watched Ramp and the linemen scream their way through fifty-pound flys while the ironheads nodded.

In the shower room, they checked each other out. You never look so good as after a heavy workout, thought Matt. Everything looks bigger. Tyrell's shoulders were black bowling balls, his butt was stone. Imagine if he juiced with us. Tyrell said he was afraid of losing quickness. They'd argued over that. Olympic sprinters used steroids and growth hormone all the time. But Tyrell said they just blew ahead straight while he needed to cut and fade. Matt thought it might be about money. Tyrell never had much. In the city, Tyrell lived with his grandmother in a housing project.

Tyrell split when they headed for Monty's office behind the one-way glass mirrors. You couldn't see in but Monty could see out. He opened the door before Matt knocked.

"You're gonna love this stuff," Monty said as they filed in. He closed the door. "I got a new supplier, Canadian. He puts together stacks for NFL players."

"How much?" asked Brody.

"For you guys, I'm sticking with the old prices. This batch is $220."

Monty took a FedEx box out of a metal locker and began unpacking bottles. He spread a clean white towel across the top of his desk and laid out the bottles, syringes, needles, and alcohol swabs. Monty was in his forties, but he still had the shape of a bodybuilder even if the muscles had shrunk and softened. As usual, Matt was fascinated by his precision. Monty stripped the paper wrappers off the syringes, screwed on the needles, and pulled off their plastic guards with his teeth. He stabbed a needle through the rubber top of a bottle and slowly drew out the oily yellow liquid.

Pete groaned softly. He was solid and dependable on the field, but he always started sweating and swaying about now. Still, he hadn't fainted in more than a year.

Monty flicked a forefinger against a syringe and pushed a drop of liquid through the tip of the needle. "Who's first?"

"Matt's number one in my book," said Pete, raising a middle finger. He was white as a ghost but trying to keep it together.

"Grab your ankles, Matt." Monty always said that.

Matt loosed the drawstring on his shorts and let them drop to his flip-flops. No underwear in this weather. He bent over the desk. Monty slapped him high on the buttock to numb the skin and rubbed it with alcohol. Matt felt a pinch and a sting as he drove in the needle, then the sensation of something cold sliding into the big muscle.

"This is the Decadurabolin," said Monty. "Stacked with testosterone. Gonna rip you big-time, man. It's the all-pro

7

cocktail. I'll give you some Danabol pills, too."

Monty slipped out the needle and pressed the swab on the puncture site. Matt imagined the steroids rushing through his system, finding the muscles, healing them, building them, making them stronger.

Brody pushed Pete forward. He was shivering as he gripped the edge of the desk. Pete closed his eyes as Monty drilled him. The weekly injections turned Pete to jelly, even though his big, soft backside swallowed the needle. Brody didn't seem to notice the shot.

Watching them, Matt felt a surge of brotherhood. He felt even closer to them in here than in the weight room or on the field. Taking the shots proved their commitment to the team and to each other. We'll do whatever it takes to get bigger, get better, to win.

There was a knock at the door, then Ramp's voice. "Yo, Doctor Monty. Ready for the men?"

"Just a minute." Monty grinned at Matt. "No excuses now. Gonna kick some this season, right?"

"Right," said Matt. This is our time, he thought.

ROBERT LIPSYTE has been an award-winning sportswriter for *The New York Times* and was the Emmy-winning host of the public affairs show *The Eleventh Hour*. He is the author of a number of acclaimed novels, including THE CONTENDER, THE BRAVE, THE CHIEF, WARRIOR ANGEL, ONE FAT SUMMER, and RAIDER'S NIGHT. He is also the recipient of the Margaret A. Edwards Award honoring his lifetime contribution in writing for teens. Robert Lipsyte lives in New York. You can visit him online at www.robertlipsyte.com.

For exclusive information on your favorite authors and artists, visit www.authortracker.com.